HERO IN MY BED

A OPPOSITES ATTRACT ROMANCE

PIPER SULLIVAN

Copyright © 2019 by Piper Sullivan

All rights reserved.

No part of this book may be reproduced in any form or by any electronic or mechanical means, including information storage and retrieval systems, without written permission from the author, except for the use of brief quotations in a book review.

Sign up to my Exclusive Romance Connoisseurs' Club to receive my Free Romance, Her Fake Fiancé Billionaire Boss.

CHAPTER 1
NINA

Some people might think working as a bartender in a small-town bar would give me the inside track on all the gossip that could be found in a town the size of Tulip, Texas.

Those people would be wrong, though. As it turns out, booze does not loosen lips nearly as effectively as a stare-down from a blue-haired old lady. That's right — all the gossip was carefully released in a steady trickle by a group of three old women ranging in age from seventy-something to the high end of eighty.

At twenty-five, I didn't qualify for their inner circle, never mind that I was an outsider who'd only been a resident of Tulip for the past seven months. Who knew how long it would take before I became a local, not that I'd planned to stick around that long.

Maybe.

It was late afternoon and the Black Thumb was mostly empty, now that the lunch rush was over. But Janey Matheson, photographer extraordinaire, held court at one of the booths that split the restaurant seating area from the pool tables, dartboards, and foosball tables. And since the daytime waitresses had all left after counting their tips, it was up to me to make sure her crowd received their pitcher of margaritas and round of tequila shots.

"Here we go, ladies," I announced, unloading my tray onto the table.

"Thanks, Nina." Janey flashed a bright smile, her perky ponytail bouncing just from the force of her words. "Hey, would you sign up to be part of a bachelor and bachelorette auction? It's for a good cause."

I frowned back at her cheerful face. As nice as the people in Tulip were, they were also manipulative as hell. One kind word, and you were signed up to judge a meatloaf cooking contest and a senior beauty pageant.

"Hell, no. Guys can be weird and creepy and totally pervy. Best to put the control and the bidding in the hands of women."

She beamed another smile my way, dimples winking from both cheeks, giving her a girl-next-door appeal I was sure the men of Tulip appreciated. "You are a genius, Nina. An absolute genius."

I mean, *I* thought so but, big surprise, so did Janey. "You said bartender wrong," I deadpanned, which for some reason made all the women at the table erupt in laughter. "Besides, I'm more of a look-but-don't-touch kind of girl when it comes to men."

Janey's raven brows rose in surprise. "So, you're... celibate?" She gasped, as though the idea was so far-fetched that she just couldn't believe it.

"Since I moved here, yeah. And I'm fine with that."

Honestly, I was. Sure, men had their purpose, but so far I hadn't found one worth keeping, and until I did, celibacy was fine with me. "Batteries can do wonders for a girl's disposition."

She tapped her chin, her gaze thoughtful. "You do make a valid point, but men are just so big and strong and... delicious." As Janey seemed lost in her own thoughts, I started to wonder if there was anyone in particular who put that wistful look on her face. "Oh. My. God. You really *are* a genius, Nina!"

I let that compliment sink in, because I didn't get them all that often from anyone other than myself. "You're going to sell vibrators, instead of the men of Tulip?"

For the past three months, everyone in town over the age of fifteen had been trying to come up with the perfect fundraiser to repair the town center's statue-fountain-garden structure, which featured the town founder Tulip Worthington.

"No, we're going to do a calendar. A big ol' beefcake calendar, showing off the men of Tulip."

I shrugged. "I'd buy one." As the saying went, they grew 'em big down in Texas and the men here seemed to be especially big, even for Texas.

"Oh, this is good. *So* good," Janey muttered to herself, whipping out a red, white, and blue notebook with a cover that looked like a pair of distressed jeans. After a minute or two of furious writing, she was on her feet and rushing out the door.

I turned to the rest of the women and grinned. "Let me know if you ladies need anything else."

"Salt, please."

"Coming right up." The thing I loved most about Texas was how friendly and open everyone was. Sure, I was still an outsider, but the people here said 'please' and 'thanks' automatically, never making me feel like the service worker I was.

The doors flew open and Janey breezed back in, smacking a couple twenty-dollar bills on the bar with a wide smile. "Sorry, and thanks." Then, she was gone again, leaving the Black Thumb just a little quieter and dimmer than before.

My three occupied tables all had drinks while they waited for their late lunch orders to arrive. I slid behind the bar and busied myself with the boring part of my job – wiping down the counters, restocking empty bottles of booze, and checking the levels on the kegs.

The last task I needed to finish before my shift ended was cutting more garnish for the cocktails the good people of Tulip rarely ordered. But I liked working at the Black Thumb and I liked my boss, Buddy, even if he was a bit crusty and grouchy sometimes. So, I did all the tasks assigned to me without complaining.

Mostly.

"Hey, Nina, isn't your shift over already?" Buddy pushed through the swinging door off the side of the bar, leading with his gut – the result of years of enjoying too many beers and too much barbecue.

Nodding, I glanced at my watch, even though I already knew the time. "Well, my bear of a boss insists I slice these lemons as thinly as possible, so he can save some cash." I winked and Buddy doubled over with laughter, clutching his big belly until he was red in the face.

"A man don't get rich giving away stuff for free."

"Not even a drop of lemon juice?"

"Especially the little things. They want a real slice of lemon, they can order something other than a beer." It was a familiar refrain, Buddy complaining that his customers preferred cheap beer to the pricey beverages he offered. "Anyway, I didn't come out here to discuss my business strategy with you, missy."

I laughed, loving the way Buddy sometimes sounded like a librarian from the fifties. "Okay. Want to tell me why you came out, then?"

A smile that looked suspiciously like trouble crossed his face. "To remind you that you're off this weekend. Heard you got roped into helping with the Tulip's Troops annual camping trip."

Yeah, I had, and roped was exactly the right word to use. It had been a sneak attack from the one and only friend I'd made during my time in town, and somehow, I'd volunteered for the task of spending the weekend with a bunch of little girls.

"I did, and I didn't forget." I had hoped one of the attractive-but-unreliable waitresses Buddy favored would call off, but it appeared luck was not on my side.

"I'm still trying to figure out how you got them to overlook that ring in your nose and the ink on your arm," he said with a shake of his head in the direction of the colorful sleeve of tattoos traveling up my right arm.

It was a mystery to me, too. "I wish they *would* fear me, just enough that I stopped getting roped into these things."

Not that I minded much, but it always seemed to highlight my status as an outsider, as well another thing I didn't have. Family.

Buddy smacked his thigh with a laugh. "No way honey, now that they know what a soft touch you are, you're a goner. Welcome to Tulip, Nina. Now, get on out of here and enjoy the rest of your night. Maybe go out on a date or get laid, as you young people say."

I exaggerated my frown. "Laid? What's that?"

He grinned, shooing me toward the door. "Hush up and wash that apron."

"I'll do it tonight, before my date with Netflix and Reese's Famous BBQ."

"That's the most pathetic thing I've ever heard," Buddy teased. "Just wait until the blue hairs hear you're still single."

Sheriff Henderson was considerately holding the door open for me to exit, so I resisted the urge to flip Buddy the bird as I took off for the night. "Evening, Sheriff."

"Evenin', Miss Nina." He was as polite as he was

handsome. And quiet. In fact, he'd be perfect for Janey's calendar.

CHAPTER 2
PRESTON

"Wanna grab a beer tonight?" Nate Callahan asked me as we left the Search & Rescue offices on the top floor of Tulip's Emergency Services building.

"Maybe. I'll let you know, but right now, I'm beat." Search and rescue shifts were similar to fire departments — Nate and I worked three days straight with two days off, which sounded worse than it was since most of the time was spent watching for fire hazards and reposting signs.

"Beat? We had one rescue and it was two experienced hikers. What has you so tired, a woman?" Nate looked over at me and I saw the hope in his eyes quickly turn to disappointment.

"I'm just tired, that's all. We're not as young as we used to be, you know."

Nate laughed. "Speak for yourself, old man. If you change your mind, I'll be at the Black Thumb by nine. And if I don't see you there, I'll pray that you're wrapped around some fine young thing."

"Bless you," I replied sarcastically and groaned as we stepped outside. My older brother Grant was leaning against my blue Escalade, a vehicle which made me stick out like a sore thumb here in pickup truck country.

"Good luck with that," Nate said, nodding in my brother's direction. "If you do need a drink, or ten, my spare room is yours."

"Thanks, Nate. See you bright and early Saturday morning."

He sighed at the reminder of our early clock-in time, the same way he always did. "Don't remind me!"

My good mood lasted exactly as long as it took me to reach my ride. "I'm too tired for your games today, Grant."

My brother pushed off the front of the car and smoothed the sides of his designer suit, probably chosen by our mother. "Good, because I'm not here for games."

"Yeah? Then why are you here?" I couldn't remember the last time he'd stopped by to see me without an ulterior motive.

"Mom wants to see you for Sunday dinner this week."

There it was. "Then she should call and invite me," I retorted. "Or, I don't know, maybe learn my work schedule."

Which was exactly what I'd been telling our mother since she'd informed me that I was no longer part of the family, after I'd chosen S&R over law school. Not that it mattered — without an apology, I still did exactly what was expected of someone bearing the Worthington name, which meant presenting a united, picture-perfect front in public. But when it came to family get-togethers, I didn't waste my time with my own, opting instead to spend time with my best friend Ry's big group of boisterous relatives.

Grant sighed, like he was the one put out by a visit he'd initiated. "When are you going to let this go? It's getting old."

"If you hate it so much, stop dropping by uninvited." That was the problem with Grant: he thought he was always right. I thought he was just an asshole. "Trust me, these little visits aren't the highlight of my day, either."

"Mom—"

"No. Stop." I put a hand to Grant's chest, so he knew I was serious. "Mom made her decision and she's stuck to it all these years. So have I. If she wants to change things, *Mom* knows what she has to do." I didn't hate my mom, but I didn't like her much either. Even though she was a snob who respected no one's opinion but her own, I'd be willing to try if she offered up a sincere apology. "Now, if that's all you wanted?"

Grant stared at me with blue eyes about two shades lighter than mine, trying to figure me out. It was a waste of time, really, because I was a 'what you see is what you get' kind of guy. "That's all," he said, finally.

"Good. See you around." It was a lie we both told each other, because it wouldn't do for the town's favored sons to be obviously at each other's throats.

The drive home took the same fifteen minutes it always did. There was never any traffic this time of day, and few people lived on the edge of town, if they could help it. But to me, the southern edge of Tulip was perfect, and when Gary Strange had put the lot up for sale a few years back, I'd bought it and built a place overlooking the picturesque lake.

"Home sweet home." Inside the front door, I kicked off my boots and stripped down as I made my way to the bathroom. It was kind of ritualistic for me, taking a hot shower after a long shift to help gauge if I was truly exhausted or just too tired to deal with people. Even after stepping out of the steaming bathroom and changing into something more comfortable than my S&R uniform, I knew I wasn't quite ready to hit the sack, so I grabbed a couple beers and went out to my deck. To relax.

Watching the calm waters of the lake had a soothing effect on me, which I needed after another run-in with Grant the self-appointed peacekeeper of the family. It was a role he'd excelled in, until I'd thrown the proverbial wrench in our family's plan for me to, eventually, become lead counsel for Worthington Enterprises. Since then, things had broken down so much there was no longer any peace to be kept.

But here, at my home, there was always peace. Mostly because I only issued invites to friends. Close friends. My space wasn't open to women or family.

The sound of the phone ringing on the deck next to my beer broke the spell the lake had slowly begun to cast on me, and I reached over to pick it up. "Yeah?"

"Dude, your phone manners would shock an ape."

I couldn't stop the smile that spread across my face at the sound of my best friend's voice. "Ry, if an ape is calling me, he deserves my bad manners — I don't recall giving my number to any apes."

His loud, barking laugh sounded down the line. "I don't know, Pres. Maybe you've got a new type." The thing I loved about Ry was his ever-present optimism. He didn't let anything in life get him down and, without fail, started every damn day with a smile. It was a trait I admired but had no real desire to emulate. "Drinks tonight at the Black Thumb?"

"Isn't tonight Ladies Night?"

"Exactly. The ladies will show up for half-priced drinks and, by the time we get there, they'll be tipsy enough to stop pretending to be good girls."

I snorted. "We grew up with damn near every woman in town, Ry. Who do you have your eye on?"

"No one in particular." The answer came too fast to be true, but I let it slide. "So, tonight? I have news you'll want to hear."

"I'm all ears now, Ry."

"Fine, stay in the house until your cock shrivels up and dies from lack of use. See if I care."

"My cock appreciates your concern, man."

He snorted, and I could picture his smile — part annoyed and part amused. "Only because you're my brother from another mother will I indulge in any sort of gossip with you."

"Understood."

"Word around town is that Sabrina

Worthington is engaging in a bit of matchmaking, inviting nearly a dozen women to one of her infamous dinner parties. This Sunday."

I groaned. My mother Sabrina only had two children with James Worthington, my dad: Grant who was dating one of the governor's daughters, and me. Painfully, permanently single me. "That makes sense. Grant was waiting for me when I got off work, issuing an invite on Mom's behalf. I wondered why."

"Well, now we know. Preston will soon be off the market." Ry's voice boomed loudly, a sure sign that he was either alone or in the presence of one of his three sisters, who loved to pretend they had crushes on me.

"Seeing as she hasn't apologized to me, I won't be there on Sunday." And, now that I knew what her motives were, I'd make sure to be busy. "Work."

"I feel your pain, man, I really do. Even if you would be doing me a solid by going to this party and getting some numbers for me. These chicks are rich, right?"

I laughed. Ry talked a big game, but he was the proverbial nice guy. "You can go in my place, since Mom will definitely have a place setting for me." So few people went against her wishes, she'd grown to expect that the whole world would bow down at her bidding.

"I'd rather have you do the heavy lifting."

I wouldn't be doing any lifting. I'd be at work on Sunday until late in the afternoon, and then I would sleep at least ten hours. And there would be no husband-hunters to be seen. "If you don't show up in my place, you'll have to make it happen with Lefty and Righty."

Ry barked out a laugh that was way too loud and way too amused for my liking. "I always find a way. So, am I gonna see you at the Black Thumb tonight?"

I glanced down at the beer in my hand and at the other dripping condensation on the wooden slats next to me before I turned my gaze back to the lake, smiling. "Nah. I'm fine right where I am."

CHAPTER 3
NINA

Early mornings were the worst, even in a beautiful place like Tulip. But I had already agreed to this damn camping trip, which, for some reason, had to take place at the absolute ass crack of dawn. Why did I do this to myself? I knew the answer — Buddy had said it a few days ago. I was a softy. Despite my best efforts, with my badass 'don't fuck with me' persona, the ink and the piercings, I was a big ol' softy.

That, and the fact that these people were genuinely nice. Annoyingly nice, even, which made it hard to be a bitch to anyone and even harder to say no. Which is exactly how I found myself walking up First Street, Tulip's answer to Main Street, before the sun even rose.

But I wasn't prepared for a weekend filled with

seven- to nine-year-old girls. Or a weekend spent in the woods. Serial killers and other crazies didn't avoid places because they were part of the National Parks System.

Walking along First Street, right down the middle of the road, I took in the quiet beauty of the town. Brick sidewalks gave Tulip's downtown a welcoming, cozy feel, which was enhanced by colorful awnings announcing the quirky names of locally-owned businesses. There was the diner, Big Mama's Place, where you could get the best scrambled eggs on the planet. Next door was the Bloomin' Tulip Bookstore, which had been around since well before e-books were a thing, and its bright rainbow awning often gave people the wrong impression. Tulip boasted two small women's boutiques, side by side, just before you got to Bo's General Store, where you could find everything from farming equipment to blue jeans, gas grills to Brie.

It was truly a picture-perfect small town, with trimmed trees along the streets adorned with twinkle lights that flickered on as the sun's light grew dim and oversized flowerpots beside the entrances to each business. And, of course, the statue of Tulip Worthington, though it hadn't fared well during the tornado that blew through town at the start of spring.

Tulip had been a pioneer in her own right, running away from home at the age of sixteen to avoid marrying a man twice her age she didn't love. She'd thought of heading west, as many people had done at the time, but had stopped to regroup in this part of Texas and never left, after falling in love with a local farmer and helping him turn a little flower operation into what was now a multi-million dollar corporation. At least, that was the story I'd been told.

Over and over again.

Ad nauseum.

But Tulip was looking a little worse for wear — the statue, as well as the fountain and garden surrounding it, was in desperate need of a makeover.

Soon, ol' girl. Soon.

As I approached the meet-up spot just beyond Tulip's statue, I ducked into Bo's for a very large cup of coffee.

"Mornin' Nina!" Bo waved, her thick brown hair falling silkily around her shoulders. Her blue eyes were sparkling too brightly for this time of the morning.

"Hey Bo, how's it going?"

"Not too bad. Not yet, anyway. Coffee? I just got in this new hazelnut stuff that people seem to love."

She chuckled to herself as she reached for a cup and the pot of coffee behind her. "Cass refuses to get the flavored stuff, so I figured this wasn't cutting in on her business."

"Any business that can't handle a little competition is a business that will soon fail." I'd heard that enough from different employers over the years to know it was true. "And make that coffee as big as you've got. Please."

With a soft, feminine laugh, Bo set out a large disposable cup and began to pour. "Ready for your weekend in the woods?"

"You heard about that too, huh? Well, I'm not ready, not even a little bit. What if I lose a kid or something?"

"There will be other mothers with you, plus the Tulip Troop Leader. You'll be fine."

I had my doubts, but I kept them to myself and busied myself grabbing a few snack items that would make the perfect bribes for good behavior this weekend. "I guess we'll find out soon enough."

After I paid for my loot, I hurried back outside before someone thought the new chick had flaked on her responsibilities. I wasn't the first person to arrive, but thankfully, I also wasn't the last.

A few moms huddled together over coffee while their girls chatted excitedly near the bright blue school bus rented to take us to our camping spot, or close to it. I didn't know any of the women well enough to offer anything more than a wave and a nod in greeting, so I started loading my gear.

"Hey Nina, glad you could make it."

I smiled as I backed out of the seat I'd chosen all the way in the back of the bus, turning in the direction of my friend Max's voice. "I'm here," I confirmed, "and I'm prepared for just about anything."

Maxine Nash had been the first person to befriend me on my second day in Tulip. With curly red hair, big green eyes, and enough curves to make Sofia Vergara jealous, Max was a vibrant single mother who cooked the best food I'd ever had the fortune of tasting. "You'll be fine. The girls love you and they listen to you, which puts my mind at ease."

As the official leader of the Tulip Buds, the name assigned to the youngest group of Tulip's Troops, the safety of everyone involved in this trip fell on Max's shoulders — which is how I got roped into this in the first place.

While I had my doubts about the girls, with plenty of other moms around I figured I was the designated fun grownup. By the time the bus was loaded with gear and the girls, though, tension started to creep in.

As we left the town of Tulip behind and the girls were on their thirtieth bottle of perfume on the wall, I was dancing on the edges of a full-blown panic attack. It was a special kind of torture, one that ended only when the bus came to a stop in one of the parking lots outside the seemingly endless national park.

"Thank god," I whispered to Max, who shook her head with a soft chuckle.

"That wasn't too painful, right?"

Easy for her to say, since she was used to the chaos of having kids around. Between her adorable daughter and her friends, the stress of being a caterer and business owner, Max thrived on challenge. I, on the other hand, had been alone for most of my life — this kind of activity was new to me.

After my father died, my mom spent less and less time at home, until finally, she just stopped coming home altogether. My Uncle Rudy stepped in and raised me from the time I was seven until he died after I turned twelve.

I spent the next three years bouncing from foster home to foster home, dealing with money grubbers, perverts, abusers, and the occasional genuine people before I called it quits. Unwilling to continue being tangled up in the system, I stayed under the radar for a few years, got my GED, and left St. Louis behind for good. So yeah, my life was mostly quiet, and this was... not.

"Not if you gave birth to one of the little tone-deaf divas, I suppose."

"What about me, Nina?" Max's seven-year-old daughter looked up at me with big brown eyes, her lopsided red ponytail swinging behind her. "Am I tone deaf, too?"

Callie was quite possibly the cutest little girl in town, with that generous sprinkling of freckles dusted across her nose and cheeks. "I heard one voice that sounded pretty damn good." She gasped at my language, and I shrugged as I crouched down to bring my face level with hers. "I thought it was me, at first, but then I remembered I can't sing, so it must've been you."

"Really?" The awe in her voice gripped my heart and I smiled.

"Yep. I'm sorry to have to tell you that you have terrible taste in music though, squirt."

She laughed. "Hey, I'm a kid. You can't say that!"

"I just did. Now, grab your gear so we can get this show on the road."

Not that Callie or any of the other buds offered much help when it came to putting up tents or setting up camp, but they were the troops and we had to let them earn their badges.

Or try, anyway.

I'd only been at this camping thing for about six hours, but other than a headache, things were going well. Two girls were on time-out in their tents for mocking Bailey, a quiet seven-year-old with white-blond hair who had just moved to town.

Was it wrong to call nine-year-old girls, bitches? Probably, so I kept the thought to myself.

The kids sat around the fire in groups of two or three, chatting with more animation than any human needed. Max and Callie were huddled together, watching another girl working on getting a smaller fire going. Bailey sat on the other side of the big fire, all alone, so I figured I'd better set a good example by trying to include her. "Hey kid, what are you doing here all by yourself?"

She shrugged, barely looking up as I took a seat on the log beside her. "Just watchin'."

"I know what you mean."

"You do?" She looked over at me cautiously.

I nodded. "Of course, I do. I moved here recently too, and it's hard to find out where you belong in a place where the people have known each other since the day they were born."

"I'm not good at making friends," Bailey confessed.

"Me, either. Max was the first person to befriend

me." She'd accosted me in the grocery store, looking for someone to act as a guinea pig for her new recipes. From then on, she hadn't let me get away with *not* being part of the community.

"Callie, too," Bailey said sadly. She was a shy girl who probably relied on having friendly, outgoing friends more than she should. "I like your tattoos."

"Thanks, you're one of the few people around here who does." Everyone stared. Half of them probably thought I was some disgraced biker chick, but they were far too polite to say it out loud. "What badges do you plan to earn this weekend, Bailey?"

She shrugged. "I already know how to start a fire, so I guess first aid, environmental stewardship, and nature identification?"

"You guess?"

"Yeah. I'm good at following directions, but some of them need you to have a buddy and I don't have one. Callie and Toni are already buddies."

Well, shit. How did parents walk around all the time with their hearts bleeding and breaking for their kids? "Then I guess we'll be buddies, and that's good news for you — I don't need any badges. You can teach me all this stuff and probably get yourself some kind of teacher badge."

Bailey giggled, but her face still looked serious. "Thank you."

"Anytime, kid. Now, let's get over there before all the marshmallows are gone." I stood and held out my hand, waiting patiently because I knew exactly what it meant to be a stubborn little kid. Plus, I was pretty confident I could out stubborn her any day of the week. "Well?"

"Fine." Sighing, she took my hand and let me tug her to the other side of the campfire where she grabbed two sticks, marshmallows, and s'mores ingredients.

Then, she retired back to the other side of the fire. I grinned. Bailey was my kind of kid.

CHAPTER 4
PRESTON

Days off were precious to me, because of how the NPS configured schedules. Working three days on with two days off meant I had to get everything — including cleaning, shopping, running errands, and even doctor's appointments — done in those two days. There was no relaxing on my days off until all the busy work was out of the way.

Today was a rare full day of no work — I'd gotten everything done yesterday, which meant the entire day was mine. I didn't plan to do a damn thing, other than watch TV and maybe finish building the bookshelf I'd started months ago.

Even *that* was a big fat maybe.

But the sound of the doorbell over the hard rock music blaring from my stereo put a major kink in my plans. Resisting the temptation to pretend I didn't hear it, I pulled the door open to see Ry standing on the front porch. "What are you doing here?"

"Good to see you too, butthead." He punched my shoulder and walked right inside, like it was his house instead of mine — something we'd been doing since we were boys. "I figured you were over here wallowing, and I thought you might want some company."

"Not really." I grinned at Ry as he surveyed the room. "But, since you brought beer, you can stay."

"Gee, thanks." His sardonic tone pulled a smile from me and he glanced around the living room at the empty pizza box and beer bottles that littered the coffee table. "Look at this dump. Your anal retentiveness must be on the fritz," he teased, pounding on my back like it was an old school TV.

"Stop that." I smacked his hand away and he laughed, following me to the kitchen. "I wasn't in a cleaning mood this weekend, sue me."

"It's not like you can't afford a cleaning lady."

"You know why I don't." My trust fund had been released when I turned twenty-five and, since it had been put in place by my grandfather, mom couldn't use it to punish me or manipulate me to get her way.

"I *know,* but I still don't understand." Ry shook his head, but dropped the subject. "Maybe you could get me a cleaning lady, then? My birthday is coming up."

"In, like, six months," I shot back and made my way to the kitchen.

"Still coming up," he explained with a shrug and shoved the six pack in the fridge, pulling out two already cold beers and handing one to me. "You really aren't going to your mom's dinner party this weekend?"

Everyone in Tulip knew about Sabrina Worthington's infamous dinner parties and thought it was a privilege to get an invite. Me excluded.

"If Mom can so easily dismiss me from the family for my choices, she can be a damned adult and apologize if she wants our relationship to change. Until that happens, I'll only show up to public events."

"You think the town doesn't notice?"

I was sure they did; the main currency in Tulip was gossip. "You think I care?" It had hurt at first, admittedly, that one little difference of opinion had pretty much cost me my family, but as time wore on, the pain had turned to anger and frustration to the point that it had stopped mattering to me. "Besides, I'm happy where I am."

"Are you?"

"Hell, yes. All those charity functions where

more money goes to putting on the event than to the actual charity, the gorgeous empty shells of women groomed to become trophy wives, the constant talk of business, vacations, and material bullshit — no, thank you."

"Let's go back to these gorgeous empty shells for a moment."

We both laughed at that, having experienced our fair share of girls "slumming it" with men they'd never consider husband material: an EMT and a search and rescue worker.

"Did you finally strike out with little miss mysterious?" Ry's mystery crush had him all tied up, but he still wouldn't say anything about her. Trying to guess her identity had become my favorite pastime.

"Nah, she's going out of town this weekend. Soon though, I'll ask her."

"You've been saying that for months." Ry glared at me and I chuckled, nodding toward the back deck. "Come on, those steaks aren't gonna cook themselves."

Ry pushed past me to the spice rack his baby sister had given me as a housewarming gift. "Thank goodness for Shelby or we'd be eating plain beef." He pulled out a few small glass bottles and sprinkled various seasonings on both sides of the meat before pushing it aside. "I know you have fries in the freezer; pop'em into the oven."

I knew the drill. This was our routine whenever we hung out: steak and fries, with beer on my deck. "Happy, chef?"

"Ecstatic. So, tell me how the Worthington clan is handling the fact that the whole town wants to help repair Tulip's Tribute?"

"No clue. Contrary to what my mother thinks, the entire world doesn't revolve around what she wants. Besides, the town council took it out of her hands," I told him with a smile. "Probably because she thinks throwing money at every problem puts her in charge of it all."

"Including your love life."

"Especially that," I groaned. Just thinking about her interference pissed me off. "This dinner party will be the perfect time for her to learn another valuable lesson — if I do choose to settle down, it will be with a woman *I* choose for reasons *I* deem important."

Besides, how Mom thought she could get one of her society girls to marry a man who wore a uniform to work and climbed rough terrain for a living was beyond me.

"You know she thinks you'll give in at the last minute? She said as much to the Potluck Patrol."

That was the name we'd given to the trio of town gossips who were the first to show up on your doorstep to welcome you, console you, or celebrate your achievements with various potluck offerings.

"I can't worry about what my mom thinks or I'll actually lose my mind."

"Well, how about a different mom?" Ry offered. "Mine's having a barbecue next weekend and she's demanding your famous sweet potato salad, along with your presence."

I had to smile as my head nodded automatically. Betty Kemp was the mother I always wanted. At five-foot-nothing and weighing a buck oh five, she was bossier than any CEO or drill sergeant. "I'll be there."

"Maybe I ought to have Ma share her secrets with Sabrina."

"Do it and I'll put super glue in your shampoo."

Ry frowned and raked a hand through his thick brown wavy hair — his pride and joy. "You fight dirty."

"Don't you forget it," I confirmed, aiming the tongs his way.

"Like I could," he said, raising a dramatic hand to his side. "I still have the scars to prove it."

"First of all, we were twelve. And you lost your balance."

His lips twitched; he knew it was true. "That's revisionist history and you know it. You totally pushed me."

"I tried to save your dumb ass!" I'd nearly fallen from that same tree in my effort to keep Ry from dropping about twenty feet to his death. Luckily, he'd only ended up with a badly broken arm. "And, if I recall, that cast got you a date with Mary Sue Markham."

Ry smiled broadly, his gaze wistful. "Yeah, that was a damn good three weeks. One more and I'd have gotten some boob action."

I pulled open the doors that led to *my* pride and joy — the teak deck I'd spent a full month building, sanding, and staining. "If you want, I can break your arm again and you can get another three weeks with Mary Sue. I hear she's between husbands right now."

Ry shuddered as he pulled open the lid of the grill and started it up. "No thanks. She's way too fertile, and I can't see myself with Mary Sue in sickness and in health and all that crap."

"And the ladies say romance is dead," I teased. He flipped me off and grabbed the steaks, tossing them on the hot grill. "Can't imagine why they're not flocking to you."

"Yeah? You're rich, buddy, and they're not flocking to you, either."

"Thank goodness for that." The last thing I needed was a repeat of college and the subsequent year of law school, with eager coeds looking to land a rich husband. It was exhausting, fending them off and trying to figure out if a girl was into me for me or just for the money I would inherit a few years after graduation. "When I'm ready, I'll find a girl."

Ry smirked, closing the lid on the grill as he popped open his beer and took a long slug. "Or maybe, she'll find you."

"In this town full of women I've known since birth? Unlikely."

"Famous last words, my friend. Famous last words."

CHAPTER 5
NINA

By ten o'clock, all the little campers were counted — twice — and snug in little sleeping bags decorated with unicorns, princesses, and in Bailey's case, the cosmos.

The night was still and quiet, save for the occasional sound of little giggles from the older girls who hadn't yet tired themselves out. I could hear it all from my spot by the smoking campfire, which had been extinguished earlier but still emanated heat, allowing me to snuggle into my own sleeping bag and stare up at the gorgeous dark sky.

For a while, the velvet indigo expanse was clear and bright, with stars winking at me from high above. But after a few moments, thick clouds started rolling in, and a crack of thunder sounded. Close. Too close to mean anything good. Even though the tents were all waterproof, tension and worry crept under my skin.

"Nothing to worry about," I assured myself as lightning illuminated the sky. The storm was close, and it was moving in fast.

A fat drop of rain fell right between my eyes and I sat up, glancing quickly around the campsite to see if everything looked the way it should. My anxiety ratcheted up a notch as the raindrops started to fall — slow and fat at first, but by the time I had rolled up my sleeping bag, the rain was coming down like thousands of tiny razor blades, pelting my skin through the thin t-shirt I'd somehow thought would be the ideal nightwear. "Shit!"

"Nina, what are you doing out here?"

I looked over my shoulder at Max, who'd emerged from her tent with a worried expression on her face. "I was star-gazing, until the clouds rolled in."

She nodded absently, scanning the campsite. "We'll need to do another count, make sure none of the girls decided to go exploring in the night."

"Okay. You count left to right and I'll count right to left, make sure our numbers match up?"

Max was worried, it was written all over her face and her demeanor. "Okay. See you in a bit." I watched her walk away, shoulders slumped against the pounding rain as her feet moved at a steady clip.

It took us a couple of minutes to count the campers, peeking carefully inside each tent so as not to wake or worry them. But when I reached the far left side of our campsite, I'd counted one missing girl.

It was my worst fear. I'd just moved to this town, and now I'd lost a kid.

In the damn woods. During a thunderstorm.

"Nina, we're a camper short!" Max's voice sounded panicked.

"I know." I sighed and wiped the rain off my face. "Bailey's missing."

Max hugged herself tight around her middle, anxiety and fear radiating off her. "It's not just that — there's a flash flood warning and we're less than a mile from the Red Clay Basin." At my blank look, she clarified, "It means we'll be standing in a big ass river if we don't get out of here fast."

Shit. Before I could even ask what to do next, the sky opened up and began dumping gallons and gallons of water on top of everything in sight. "You get all the other moms to help pack up the girls. I'll see if I can find Bailey."

The little girl was out there on her own and no matter how smart she was, her fifty-pound frame would not be able to withstand the rush of water that was headed our way.

"Wait!" Max's frantic voice stopped me in my tracks, and I turned to face her. "You can't go out there alone, Nina. It's dangerous."

"Imagine how much worse it is for a scared little girl, Max. Someone has to go after her, and I'm the only one who doesn't have anyone else depending on me."

It was a sad fact, but it *was* a fact. My last living relative had died more than a decade ago, and in that time, I hadn't formed any lasting connections. There was no one out there who might miss me if I didn't come back.

"That's bullshit and you know it." I recognized Max's angry voice.

"Let's argue about it if I come back, yeah?" Before she could say anything else to discourage or dissuade me, I pulled out my flashlight and took off in the direction of the basin, knowing there was plenty of foliage and wildlife to draw a little explorer to that exact spot.

As I ventured further away from camp, the night seemed to grow darker and I pushed down the fear and panic that threatened to overwhelm me. There was no time to be afraid. "Bailey? Can you hear me?" I closed my eyes and held my breath, hoping to hear a small cry or a child's yell over the rain, or at least through it.

Nothing.

I pushed deeper into the darkness, into the thickest part of the forest where the key to Bailey's badges would be. "Bailey!" I strained to listen to a reply, but instead, I heard a loud, unidentifiable crack followed by fuzzy white noise. No, not white noise — water. Lots and lots of water. "Bailey!"

The further I walked the higher the water became, until it was ankle deep. I trudged ahead, calling out the little girl's name at the top of my lungs until I came upon an open space surrounded by rocks. Boulders, really. Then, I heard something. "Help! Somebody help me, please."

"Bailey! Bailey, can you hear me?"

It was too dark to see anything at all; the clouds were too thick for the moonlight to peek through. "Bailey!" I screamed again.

The water rose faster and faster. Too fast.

"Help!" Bailey's voice was closer now. I searched the area with my flashlight. "Right here! Help, I'm right here!"

The ray of light allowed me to catch a brief flash of a waving arm in the distance, but all the water made my movements slow and sluggish.

The dirt had become a thick mud that felt more

like quicksand, and every step was an effort. "I see you, Bailey, keep talking!"

"Nina! I'm scared!"

"Me too, kid. But we've gotta be brave, okay?"

As soon as the words left my mouth, the earth dropped from beneath my feet and I slid under the water. I struggled to find the ground, and after several tries, I knew it was pointless. Kicking my legs behind me, I pushed back above the surface and sucked in a gulp of air. "Bailey?"

"Are you okay, Nina?" Her voice was closer but somewhere to my left, and I had to change direction through the thick, muddy water.

"So far, so good, kid." It took me a few minutes, but I finally located Bailey, thanks to her flickering flashlight in one hand. With her other hand, she was holding onto something I couldn't quite see. When I made it over to her, Bailey's little face broke into a wide grin.

"Nina! I'm so happy to see you!"

I snorted as I tried to wrap my arm around whatever she was using to anchor herself, but failed. "Given the circumstances, I'm sure you are."

Reaching out again, I banged my knuckles against something hard and unyielding. Stone.

Her laugh turned into a cough, and she started

spitting up some water that made me worry. "I'm scared, Nina."

"I know, I am, too. Fear isn't gonna help us right now, though, so I need you to push it down."

"How do I do that?" The flashlight fell from her hand and I caught it before it hit the water.

I struggled to grab onto the top of the big ass boulder Bailey clung to. Instead, my hand caught on a pointy edge, and I bit back a wince of pain as it dug into my palm. "Just keep telling yourself that your strength is stronger than your fear."

Bailey squeezed her eyes shut and repeated the words over and over in a soft whisper, then snapped them back open and stared at me as she asked hoarsely, "Are we going to die, Nina?"

Jeez, kids sure got right to the quick, didn't they? "No, I don't think so," I told her honestly, even though I didn't feel completely sure about it myself. "But we have to believe we will, because I'm not sure either of us has the muscle to hold onto this rock forever."

Her giggle sounded sweet and musical to my ears, and I had a sudden thought that if it was the last sound I ever heard, that wouldn't be so bad. "You said we were strong."

"We are. Mentally strong, but physically, I think

the water and this rock might have us beat." Even as the words fell from my lips, Bailey began to slip.

"Nina!"

My arm shot out to grab the girl, and we both fell to the water as my hand wrapped around the fabric of her night shirt. "Nina, I—"

"Hold on to me and don't let go. No matter what, okay?"

Bailey nodded, her green eyes wide and terrified. "Okay."

"All right." I sucked in several deep breaths and let them out slowly, mustering up all the energy I could find to climb back up the rock with an additional fifty pounds on my back. It was slow going, and my muscles screamed their misery at the fire burning with every move.

My breaths huffed out of me with more force than someone of my age and weight should require, but finally, that rocky point dug into the center of my palm and I hung on with everything I had. "You all right back there, kid?"

"Yeah, I-I-I think so."

"Good." I held onto the rock as hard as I could while the rain pelted us from all sides and thunder cracked overhead. My heart raced with the speed of a stallion and my arms trembled from exhaustion, but I kept my grip. Bailey was counting on me.

"Do you have a boyfriend, Nina?"

"Nope."

"I don't, either," she said sullenly.

"You're too young for a boyfriend."

She giggled. "That's what my mom says. too. But you're not too young."

Ouch. "No, I'm not too young but I'm... difficult." It was a word that had been used to describe me on more than one occasion, even by my Uncle Rudy who I knew loved me dearly. "I'm sure I'll find one."

Eventually. I didn't really believe it, but there was no point in sharing that with a little heart that had yet to be broken beyond repair.

The sound of more water rushing broke through the steady noise of rain bouncing off rocks and trees, and my grip tightened. Moments later, we were both swept away by the flood.

CHAPTER 6
PRESTON

"You're really not interested in any of them women roaming around town in hopes of becoming Mrs. Preston Worthington?" Nate's eyes showed as much shock as his voice held when I shook my head.

"Not even a little bit. If I have to spend the next fifty years with a woman, I'd rather it be one that I can stand being around. At least."

Truthfully, though, I hoped for more than that. Love, affection, attraction, and maybe even genuine like. "Feel free to attend in my absence."

Nate shook his head firmly. "No thanks. High maintenance women are not my thing."

"Yeah, we're all taking bets on whether or not you have a woman tucked away in the park some place." With his short-cropped red hair and a matching beard, Nate looked every bit the lone mountain man he portrayed himself to be. He hadn't dated anyone seriously in the four years we'd worked together for the NPS.

His chuckle was loud and booming, and he even threw in a knee smack for good measure. "If you find her, let me know. Hell, I'd love a woman who was just as happy being out in nature as she was at a dinner party or a football game."

"You attend football games?" This was Texas, after all, and football was king, but I'd never seen Nate at a single game.

"Not yet, but I could."

We shared a laugh, but the crackle of the radio interrupted with a call and we were both instantly on high alert. Nate picked up the phone that automatically connected to the dispatch officer, his expression growing darker by the second. "Team two responding."

"What's up?" In unison, we rose quickly to our feet, grabbing our S&R bags and heading out to the green and gold truck.

"Tulip's Troops are caught out in the rain and there's a flash flood crashing through the basin at the south end of the park," he relayed. "Two campers are missing and that's all we got. Let's go."

It took us less than ten minutes to get to the site,

where we found ankle deep water that was quickly rising. Maxine Nash ran up to me, a little girl quick on her heels. "Oh, thank god you're here, you have to find them!"

I put my hands on her shoulders to make sure her panicked eyes locked with mine. "I need you to calm down and tell me what you know."

Max sucked in a deep breath, closed her eyes, and let it out. When she opened them again, she spoke like the no-nonsense woman she'd proven to be over the years. "When the first drop of rain fell, Nina and I did a bed check to count all the girls. One was missing — Bailey." Tears welled in her eyes and she put her fist to her mouth in distress. "I shouldn't have let her go off on her own, dammit."

"Probably not," Nate agreed matter-of-factly, shrugging indifferently when I glared at him.

"I didn't want her to, but she insisted, saying no one was waiting at home for her, which is total bullshit. But…" Tears began to drip down her cheeks. "I could have gone with her but I thought of Callie and I just… couldn't." She held the little girl — who I now assumed was Callie — close and something like sympathy crept under my skin. Now wasn't the time.

"It's fine; just tell us where she went, Max."

She pointed in the direction of the basin and I

groaned as Callie stepped forward and tugged on my rain jacket. "Bailey is trying to get her wildlife badge, so I think she went to the small lake where there are deer and stuff for animals to eat and drink."

I dropped down on my haunches and covered her small shoulder with one hand. "Thanks, Callie. That's a big help." Standing back up, I turned to Max. "Now, you both need to get on the bus where it's warm and dry. The driver will move you away from the flooding and we'll follow with the other two when we find them."

I made sure to say 'when,' not 'if' — it seemed like Nina meant a lot to these women. I didn't know much about her, other than that she was a relatively new waitress at the Black Thumb.

"This could get messy," Nate admitted, striding up next to me as we watched Max and her daughter jog to the bus.

"Stupid woman shouldn't be trying to be a hero." I hoped she wouldn't lose her life and the kid's, but there was no time to worry about that. We had to find her in the pouring rain, flash flooding, and absolute blackness.

"You'd expect a woman to leave a little girl alone to possibly drown? Even you're smarter than that." Nate clapped me on the back with a good-natured chuckle and we moved as one, calling out their names and using high-powered flashlights to search the area carefully.

Anything could happen in this kind of flooding — one moment, the rain seemed little more than an annoyance, and the next, it washed away everything. Trees, bushes, shrubs, overflowing ponds, and lakes. People and houses, too. It could wash away everything during the night and, in the morning, leave a vibrant, lively landscape with no trace of the damage it had caused. "We should head straight for the basin, 'cause it's probably half full by now."

Moving in sync, we scanned every inch of space within our sight for the two campers. By about a quarter mile from the start of the basin, we were in waist high water.

"Stop! Wait!"

Nate's flashlight caught the streak of red first. "There," I called out to him. "Don't worry, we're here to help."

"No shit," Nina called out blandly. "The ground dips significantly in about twenty feet. I went under and my feet couldn't find the ground!" She didn't sound panicked, which impressed me, but the worry was still clear in her voice.

"Shit," Nate groaned. "We'll need to find another path. Can't risk the water carrying us too far away."

"Yep."

"You go left and I go right?" Nate was the efficient one when it came to rescues, which was why we made a good team.

But I was the planner. "We need to stick together. That way, we both get to them and save them. *Both* of them."

Nate gave a sharp nod and tapped my shoulder, the sign he was ready to move when I was. Getting across to Nina and Bailey took longer than it should have, given the weight and rush of the water around us. "Is it me or is the water too choppy?"

"It's not just you," Nate agreed solemnly, his grip on my shoulder a little tighter as my hand landed on the rock.

"Here, grab Bailey first," Nina directed. "Bailey, don't let go until one of these guys tells you to, yeah?"

The little girl nodded, teeth chattering too hard for her to string together a sentence. "S-s-scared."

"But stronger than you are scared, right?" Nina turned her head to the side so she could see the girl nod. "Cool. These guys are professional rescuers, so they're basically super heroes."

"Really?"

I fought the urge to roll my eyes, but Nate chuckled. "Pretty much. I'm Nate and this is Preston."

Nate reached across my shoulder as Nina turned her back to us. She grabbed the little girl by the waist while I secured a rope around her. "Okay, Bailey, let go."

The little girl hesitated briefly, but did as she was told. With a bit of effort, she was safe in Nate's arms as he headed back toward flat, unmovable land.

"What about Nina?"

"I've got Nina," I shouted over the noise of the storm and the flood.

"I really hope you do," she cried, and I could hear a bit more panic in her voice now that Bailey was gone. "My hand is slipping, numb, and bleeding like crazy."

"Just hang on," I told her, but a rush of water crashed over the rock and she slipped below the surface. I instinctively reached out to grab anything I could, catching her ankle in my hand. "Gotcha!"

But Nina couldn't hear me; she was still underwater. Pulling her closer until I felt the dip of her waist, I lifted her back out. Her sputtering and cursing greeted me.

"Shit, that was close. Thanks."

"No problem. Do I need to tie you to me, or can you hang on?"

"As long as you have no pointy parts, I'm good to

go." Realizing how that comment could be interpreted, Nina let out an amused laugh. "You know what I mean. And even if you don't, that might be a bit painful for you."

I smiled as she wrapped her arms around my waist and gave a small squeeze that might have been a hug or could have been nothing more than a fear response. At the moment, my focus was on getting us the hell out of the water's path.

It took half as long to get back to stable land as it had to find the girls. Thankfully.

Nina's wobbly legs nearly dropped her to the ground when she tried to walk, so I held her arm to keep her steady. "Thank you. Both of you."

In the darkness, her hair looked black, but her eyes were such a light shade of blue they were almost clear under the emergency lights of the parking area.

"What in the hell were you thinking? You could have died out there!" It was the wrong tactic to take and I knew I was acting like it was my very first rescue, but what she'd done was stupid and dangerous.

Nina yanked angrily out of my grip and took a wobbly step back. "Excuse me? I said thank you. You can be on your way now, dude."

"It was incredibly stupid," I said, unable to help myself.

"Stupid to try and save the life of a seven-year-old child? Sounds like I should have tried to drown you before we got back to safety." Arms crossed, she turned slowly and limped away on what I now noticed wasn't just unsteady legs.

"You're hurt."

She barked out a laugh. "You couldn't hurt me if you tried, guy."

"Preston," I reminded her for some reason.

"Thanks for the rescue, but you can keep your unsolicited advice. *Preston.*"

I might have believed her if the limp hadn't gotten worse with every step, and if she hadn't cried out in pain a moment before collapsing to the muddy ground.

"Stubborn woman," I muttered. In five quick steps I was at her side, lifting her in my arms and carrying her to the truck. "You hurt your ankle and you said earlier that your hand was bleeding. Are you so pigheaded you're going to ignore solid medical advice out of spite?"

She sighed heavily and hit me with a glare so cold it made me shiver. Or maybe it was the rain. "I'll get myself to the doctor after I check on Bailey and we get back to town. It'll hold."

Before I could say another word, Max and Callie rushed to Nina's side, wrapping her — and therefore me — into a large, smothering hug.

"You scared me half to death, you big dummy," Max chided, hugging Nina tightly.

"You saved Bailey, Nina!" Callie took off in the little girl's direction and gave her the same treatment her mom had given Nina.

"Can't breathe here," Nina gasped.

Max took a step back. "I don't know whether to kill you or hug you again."

"How about you smile at me from a safe distance and get this dude to put me down?"

Folding her arms, Max glared at me. I was unmoved. "She's injured and needs medical attention," I said simply, and that was all it took to turn Nina's friend Maxine into an ally.

She sighed and stepped forward. "Let Preston help you, Nina."

"I can help myself." She turned to me and once again I was struck by those beautiful blue eyes. "Not that I'm ungrateful, but I can get to the doctor on my own. It's not an emergency, which means it can wait until I get some dry clothes and my car."

"The bus will drop you at the ER, Nina, no problem."

Nina opened her mouth to refuse the help, but I

spoke first. "Perfect. Give me your keys and I'll get you clothes and your car."

She laughed again. "First of all, I don't know you, and there's no way in hell I'm letting you into my house to rifle through my panty drawer."

"And, second?" I asked, amused by her feisty attitude. Women rarely took that tone with me, but Nina didn't seem at all concerned about coming across as offensive.

"Second," she added, "*nobody* drives my car."

It was a sweet little ride, a royal blue 1965 Mustang GT convertible — plenty of car for such a small woman. "Can't blame a guy for trying."

She rolled her eyes as I got her settled on the front seat of the bus with her leg elevated and gauze wrapped around her bleeding hand. "Thanks for not being too big a jerk about this," she said, softly.

I smiled. She had no idea.

CHAPTER 7
NINA

If there was one place I never wanted to spend any time at all, it was the hospital. Not that there was anything wrong with the West Texas General Hospital, located a short twelve miles from Tulip, I just didn't want to be there. The nurses were a little too chipper, but the doctor had seemed competent for the five minutes I'd seen him before he ordered me to get X-rays on my right ankle and right hand.

Two hours later, my bones had been photographed with both an X-ray and an MRI, and I sat in an uncomfortable, semi-private room located in the emergency department, waiting. And waiting. And waiting.

My patience had worn thin. My nerves were still a little frazzled and there was a better-than-good chance I was suffering from a mild case of shock, judging by my cold, clammy skin, racing heart, and slight feeling of nausea. Or, maybe it was just the excitement of the past few hours. Either way, I was totally fucking over it.

I couldn't even get any rest because of all the noises that surrounded me. Machines beeping, nurses gossiping, impatient parents demanding quicker treatment for their sick or injured kids. The fluorescent lights weren't helping, either, so I lay back, closed my eyes, and flung my forearm over my face to block out as much of it as I could.

The last time I'd set foot in a hospital was the day I said goodbye to Uncle Rudy. I'd held his hand until his heart stopped beating, and vowed I'd never come back. And I wouldn't have, if not for my stubborn friend and a bossy rescue worker.

"How are we feeling, Ms. Ryland?" The young ER doctor, Dr. Cahill, strolled in with a Hollywood superstar smile on his handsome face. His thick, curly black hair stood up messily, and I wondered if it was a carefully cultivated look or if he was simply too busy to worry about mundane things such as his appearance.

I sighed and pushed myself up with my uninjured left hand. "We've been better, Doc. What's the verdict?"

"The good news is that none of your bones are broken." He flashed another smile that was just as stunning but held a hint of sympathy that softened it around the edges.

"Okay, what's the bad news?"

"You have a torn medial ligament in your ankle, which will require a boot for a few weeks and then rehab."

"Rehab? It's just a little swelling." Okay, sure, the swelling looked like my foot had been blown up like a balloon and it was a nasty shade of purple and blue. And yeah, it hurt like a son of a bitch, but still, it was just an ankle sprain.

"Nina." He said my name in exasperation, but his expression remained impassive. "It's a severe sprain. The shock from what happened to you tonight is probably why you can't feel how much pain you're in, but trust me, it's bad."

He leveled me with a serious look for several long seconds and I stared back, refusing to be intimidated by this smart, handsome man. They were a dime a dozen, and while he was certainly pretty to look at, he was also the reason I still sat in this miserable hospital bed.

"We'll give you a boot for your ankle and you'll have to wear it for three weeks, but not until after the first three days," he said, "where I expect you to stay off the ankle completely, except for trips to the bathroom."

"Three weeks! I can't be in a boot for that long, I work on my feet all day, Doc." Three weeks in a boot meant no work, which meant no money. "There has to be another option."

"There isn't," he informed me flatly. "And three weeks is a starting point, it could be longer. And then, there's physical therapy."

I groaned and fell back against the butcher paper covered bed. "Now, let's talk about your hand."

"Get all the good news out of the way, Doc."

It didn't really matter what he said next, because three weeks without work would eat into my savings and any longer might force me to dip into the money Uncle Rudy had left for me. Money I'd promised not to use until I figured out what the hell I would do with my life.

"The hand isn't too bad, but it will require stitches." He grinned as a nurse or intern pushed a tray beside the bed that looked an awful lot like it carried a variety of torture devices. "Probably about thirteen. It won't hurt too bad, I promise."

"Just get it done, please." I leaned back and closed my eyes, listening to his sneakered footsteps on the linoleum floor. His touch was light and his skin was warm, but none of that made the needle pricks hurt any less.

"You'll feel some tugging, Nina, but that's about it."

I nodded, keeping my eyes closed. I really didn't want to watch. The look I'd gotten at my hand earlier had been enough — seeing where the big boulder had left a star-shaped scar in the center of my hand had nearly made me sick to my stomach.

I opened my eyes just as the door pushed open and Mr. Bossy Pants himself strode into my room unannounced. "What are you doing here?"

Preston, seemingly unmoved by my tone, slung a suspiciously familiar green bag onto a chair beside the door. He shrugged with a smile that was far too disarming for my liking. "It was easier to let you think you'd won than keep arguing with you. Max let me into your place, and she packed the bag — your panty drawer remains unmolested."

The doctor snickered over my hand. I considered how to politely reprimand him for laughing at his own patient, but before I could come up with the right thing to say, he sighed and announced, "Fifteen stitches. Care to view my handiwork?"

"No thanks," I replied with a firm glare. That would have to be enough. Satisfied I'd made my point, I turned back to Preston. "Thanks for the bag. Have a good night."

"Ouch," he said, rubbing an imaginary wound at the center of his well-developed chest. "You'll need a ride home," he informed me in a take-charge tone that I did not appreciate.

"And I will find one when the time comes." If Maxine was busy, which she almost certainly would be, I'd take advantage of one of the three ride-sharing services in Tulip. "I've managed to get around this whole country on my own, but thanks for your concern," I added, in case I'd sounded ungrateful.

"You can't drive on this injury," the doctor interjected, "at least, not until after that boot comes off."

I shot him a dark look. "Isn't there a law against revealing medical information with a complete stranger in the room, Doc?"

His gaze swung from me to Preston and down to my green duffel bag before landing on me. "I apologize, but I figured he was your, uh, friend."

"I am a friend," Preston confirmed. "And the man who saved her life, along with her ride home."

"I'm sure you have paperwork to file or lost hikers to find. Don't worry about it, I'll grab a ride when I'm discharged."

He grinned, and I tried hard not to notice how

full and pink his lips were. How kissable. "Why would you do that when I'm already here?"

"Because you have to get back to work. But thanks for the bag."

"You're stubborn as hell."

He was right about that. I had to be, though, or people would walk all over me. I'd never let that happen. Not again.

"You, too. Look, I appreciate the offer, but who knows how long I'll be here. I'll just call... shit." All of my belongings were back at camp, either filled with water or dragged away by the flood. "Fine. You can loan me a quarter, or however much a payphone costs these days."

"You can make a call from here," Dr. Cahill cut in, nodding toward the phone.

I snorted. "And pay your exorbitant hospital rates? I don't think so." I turned back to Preston. "So, that quarter?"

He crossed his arms and I might have let my gaze linger on the thick, golden-brown muscles barely contained within the green shirt that was part of his uniform. Preston cut a fine figure, and his blond hair looked perfect – dry and wavy, as though he hadn't been caught up the same storm I was sure had me looking like a drowned cat. His blue eyes glittered, reminding me of the sun glinting off the ocean waves. "You don't need a quarter, just give me a holler when you're ready." To punctuate his words, he dragged the chair from beside the door and settled it, and himself, to my left.

By the time I had been provided with crutches, pain pills, and a boot for my ankle, another ninety minutes had passed and I was ready to sleep for twenty-four hours straight. "Fine," I conceded wearily. "You can drop me off at my place, if the offer still stands."

He flashed a smile as he stood and handed me the duffel bag. "That wasn't so hard, was it?"

It was harder than he knew. Relying on people wasn't my strong suit and relying on strangers wasn't something I typically even considered, but right now, I was trapped, and Preston was offering me a hand. "Thank you."

"I'll bring the car around."

I frowned. "You don't have *my* car, right?"

He grinned again and shrugged like a guilty little boy. "See you in a bit."

He didn't, thank god. The ride to my place was mostly quiet, except for the country songs playing on the radio, and I was grateful. Though I'd seen him around town, I didn't really know Preston. What I did know — that he was from the town's founding family and a rescue worker — was very little.

"Thanks for the ride, Preston."

He didn't say anything, so I shoved the door open on his big ass Escalade. Before I could climb out, his hand wrapped around my arm. "There's no way in hell you can make it up the first seven steps, never mind the second floor." He leaned forward, looking up at the old yellow Victorian that had been split into two apartments. Mine, as Preston had pointed out, was on the upper level.

"Just take me to Max's, then." I was confident she'd let me bunk on the air mattress in the craft room of her split-level home.

"She's still dealing with terrified parents of all the campers," he told me, shaking his head. "You can stay with me for the night."

"No, thanks. Why don't you take me to the nearest motel?"

"Yeah, and how do you plan to call anyone to come get you? Your phone is in a bag of rice at my place, where the rest of your stuff is drying out."

I turned to face him with a look so dark, I could have summoned Lucifer himself. "You had this all planned out, didn't you?"

"Trying to help a crazy woman who risked her life, I'm such a bastard."

Then, the big handsome asshole reached across me, brushing his muscular arm across my belly and making me gasp as he pulled the door shut. He hit the gas before I could attempt my escape. "If it'll make you feel better, Nina, you can pay me to stay at my place. I promise, the food's better than Bernie's continental breakfast at the motel on the interstate."

The way he said my name — low, slow, and sensual — was all I needed to confirm that staying with him would be a very bad idea. "Why are you pushing this? You don't even know me."

"I'm a nice guy and you need a friend," He stated plainly. He wasn't wrong, but that didn't mean I liked admitting it.

"Still. I don't know you and I'm not in the habit of sharing a home with strange men."

"Fine. My name is Preston Worthington and I work for the NPS doing search and rescue. I was born and raised here in Tulip, minus a few years for college and S&R training. I have good credit, no arrests, and you can ask anyone in town about me."

I already knew none of them would have anything bad to say. Despite his family's wealth and his model good looks, Preston seemed to be a good guy. "Do you have a girlfriend or a wife?"

It was the one piece of information that even the town gossips could only speculate on, which I found odd. And, I had to confess, pretty intriguing.

He put the gear shift in park and slid from the

truck. After jogging around the front in the way fit guys made look so easy, he pulled open my door with a grin. "Interested?"

"In whether or not some crazy chick is going to sneak in overnight and hold a knife to my throat? Hell yeah," I explained. "So?"

"No girlfriends. No wives."

"Booty calls?"

"Nope," he said with a gleam in his eyes.

"Boyfriend?"

He frowned and I laughed. "Actually, my best friend Ry *is* the only one who might show up unannounced."

"Gin Rickey with a twist of lime." It was the EMT's favorite drink, an old cocktail hardly anyone ever ordered so it had stuck with me. "He's your best friend?" I figured he hung out more with the uptight but handsome District Attorney. or some of the finance guys who lived in the city and retreated to the country only for long weekends and holidays. "Hey, what do you think you're doing? Get your paws off me!"

Ignoring me, Preston lifted me out of my seat as if I weighed nothing. Considering how tall and muscular he was, my five-foot-five frame was probably nothing, but still — a girl had her pride. "I'm helping." He smiled. *Smiled* at me, like this was some sort of game. Some flirtation.

"I have crutches to help."

"Paving the driveway is pretty low-priority on my list of things to do around here, so let's just get you to the house and then we can fight some more. Okay?"

Maybe I was being a much bigger brat that I needed to be, since he *was* offering help out of the goodness of his heart. Or, maybe it was required that Worthington family members perform a certain number of hours of good will each month. "I'm sorry. I'm tired, in pain, and no good at accepting help."

"No kidding," he muttered under his breath, snickering like I'd just told him a joke. I inhaled his scent — clean, and masculine mixed with rain and earth — and let it settle into my bones. He really was too gorgeous and too masculine. Everything about him spelled trouble. Luckily, I was only accepting his help for the evening.

Just for tonight.

"How is your pain?" The concern in his voice pulled me from my own wayward thoughts, and I turned away from the big windows overlooking the lake.

"Not great," I admitted, shrugging. "I'll survive."

"I'm sure you will, but if you're in pain, we can actually do something about it, you know?" Preston rolled his eyes, but his lips remained curled in a small smile as he pointed in this direction and that, giving me a stationary tour of his home. "You only need the bathroom since you're not supposed to be on your feet at all for the next three days."

"No need to be so bossy; I remember what the doctor said." He smirked again and folded his arms, like he thought he could wait me out. "Don't you have to get back to work?"

"You're not gonna do something stupid like try to run back home, are you?"

"As you pointed out, I couldn't navigate the gravel if I wanted to, so no. I plan to stay right here, alone, until tomorrow."

He nodded, satisfied with my response. "Good. You can take the bed, since I won't be here until tomorrow evening, anyway. I'll have Maxine or Ry bring you some food in an hour or so. Just stay off that foot."

"Yes, sir." My words were accompanied by a sarcastic salute, which produced a genuine grin that lit up Preston's whole face. It was a good face, a great face, actually, but I had no business gawking at it like it was a piece of art hanging on the wall.

"See you later, Nina."

"Thanks, Preston, for everything. Really."

He winked. "That wasn't so hard, was it?" His chuckle lingered as he made his way to the door.

"Keep talking smack and I'll put itching powder in your underwear drawer." The last thing I heard before his truck engine started up again was his deep laughter on the other side of the thick wooden door.

It was just as well. I had too much on my mind to let it daydream about a rich guy who was well and truly out of my league.

CHAPTER 8
PRESTON

The rescue of young Bailey was all the town could talk about in the days following the flood — a flood which had, as predicted, caused a great uproar only to leave behind nothing but beauty and peace, along with an influx of tourists eager to see what would bloom now that the water had revived the greenery in the park. An activity as benign as stopping for a cup of coffee was now a twenty-minute affair, as I fielded endless questions about Nina's well-being.

As for Nina, she was as much a mystery to me as she'd been since she arrived in town almost a year ago. Feisty and stubborn, Nina didn't make a damn thing easy — not even when I'd offered to cook her breakfast.

But she was also funny as hell, with a wit sharp

enough to cut through bone. And she was hot. Even though Nina Ryland was not at all my type, with tattoos all down her arm and a red gem sparkling from her left nostril, everything about her kept me fully aroused.

Her thick brown hair fell gently around her shoulders, tempting me to run my fingers through the waves to see if they felt as soft as they looked. Her light blue eyes, the color of the early morning sky, gave her an irresistible look of vulnerability, which I was sure she'd hate to hear — Nina was a tough girl. The kind of girl who didn't do vulnerability or softness, the kind of girl I usually disliked. But on her, it was damned attractive.

Or maybe I was just intrigued because she wanted nothing to do with me. Rather than be drawn to me, or at least feign interest, because of my family's wealth, it seemed to turn her off completely, which made me a total bastard for using it to get a rise out of her.

"I brought food," I called out as I let myself in the back door of my house, smiling at Nina's surprised gasp.

"There's no need for food when you're about to drive me home." She tried to stand and dropped back to the sofa, clearly frustrated. "This damn boot is driving me crazy!"

"Have you practiced walking on it?"

"Practice? I know damn well how to walk. There is no need to *practice*. This thing is ridiculous and definitely not made for walking."

Muttering grumpily to herself, Nina pushed slowly off the sofa and sighed happily when she remained upright.

"You have to practice or stay on your ass all day."

"What difference does it make, anyway? Buddy won't let me work with the boot on, even though I can walk the length of the bar and back in this thing. I mean, I'm sure I *could*, if I had a reason to practice."

I set the bag down on the counter and hurried to her side, scooping her up in my arms and setting her back down on one of the bar stools in the kitchen. "A good reason to practice might be so you can navigate those death trap steps at your apartment, unless you're finally getting used to having a roommate?"

She snorted a laugh. "You've been a great, if annoying host, Preston. But if I stay any longer, tongues will start wagging, and that's the last thing I need."

I frowned as I pulled out the Camembert, figs, prosciutto, and fresh goat cheese pizza I'd picked up at Kellyanne's Gourmet Shop. "You don't strike me as the kind of woman who gives a damn about what other people think." If she did, the tattoos and piercing might have run her out of town before she'd even signed her name on the lease.

"I don't. What I do care about is snarky mean girls leaving me shitty tips because they think I'm screwing the town golden boy." She picked up the cheese, examined the wedge from every angle, and curled her nose up into an adorable frown. "God, that smells awful."

"It does," I conceded, "but it tastes so good you'll question your sanity." I took the cheese from her and opened it, cutting a couple slices so she got one that was more cheese than rind. "Taste it and *don't* hold your breath."

Still frowning, she held the slice between two fingers for a moment, then opened her mouth and placed it on her tongue. The move shouldn't have been so sensual but good god, it was. It totally fucking was. Her thick, naturally pink lips closed, and a throaty moan pierced the silence. "Fuck me, that *is* good." She shook her head as she picked up another slice, giving it the same careful eye as she had the piece before. "Rich people are weird, but I'm starting to get it."

It was just the response I'd been hoping for. "Wait until you get your mouth on this pizza." I wiggled my eyebrows and she shook her head again, laughing.

"Now pizza, even fancy pizza, I can get excited about."

I briefly wondered what else she got excited about, but decided to save the question for another day. "So, food? Or do you want me to drive you home and watch you struggle with the stairs before you decide to come back here?"

Arms folded, glared at me as she finished chewing the cheese. "Maybe I'll struggle with the stairs and decide I want you to take me to Max's place."

That pulled another laugh from me. With her smart mouth, I never got away with anything. "I guess that's also an option, but wouldn't you rather struggle on a full stomach instead of an empty one?"

"I always prefer my stomach to be full, so that's kind of a dumb question." She slipped from the stool and limped to the fridge, pulling out two beers. "So, Preston, why search and rescue?"

"You mean instead of big business with my family?" It was a question I was asked all the time — enough that I had a pretty thick skin about it — but I'd thought Nina might be different. Maybe I was the one judging her.

She shrugged. "Or instead of becoming a cop or

a soldier, an EMT or firefighter. Doctor, lawyer, candlestick maker?"

"I spent a lot of time outdoors as a kid, hiking and fishing, swimming, and in college, I took up rock climbing. The summer before I graduated, I was part of a search party looking for two lost hikers. We finally found them huddled in a cave halfway between the ground and the top of the rock on Mount Katahdin, and I watched in awe as the S&R guys climbed up there and rescued them."

"And the rest was history?"

"Hell no," I confessed. "I managed a year of law school before I realized it was boring and I hated it, but I didn't have the guts to tell my mom. Instead, I did all the training first and then came clean."

Nina smiled, looking impressed with my deception. Admittedly, it was an odd response, but I was learning that Nina was a bit of an odd woman. "You were more worried about telling your mom than your dad?"

"Mom is all about appearances and she's the Worthington by blood, which means she cares way more than Dad." My dad had been happy for me, and he was proud of the work I did, but he didn't show it in Mom's presence.

"Did she get over it?"

I barked out a laugh as I slid the pizza into the

oven. "Nope. Kicked me out of the family, except when a photographer is around. Can't have the entire world knowing she's actually a terrible person." She wasn't truly terrible, just judgmental and overbearing, but I didn't feel like explaining that to Nina.

"Wow. Rich people really are fucked up. I think you just got more interesting, Preston."

"Thanks. I think?"

She shrugged. "I mean, it's kind of screwed up that you save people for a living and that's not somehow good enough. Sure, there are some good lawyers in the world, but there are also ones who defend rapists and corporations that kill the environment. Pretty sure you guys don't do any of that."

"We don't," I clarified, my tone deadpan. "But it wasn't part of *her* plan. None of the socialites she dreamed I would marry would be caught dead with a husband who wears a uniform to work."

Nina snorted. "Where I come from, a guy with a job and no drinking problem is considered a catch."

"Where *are* you from?" For as long as she'd been in town, there hadn't been much gossip about Nina Ryland.

"Mostly St. Louis. I lived in Cleveland until I was seven, but I don't remember much of it." Her gaze was fixed out the window, far away. I wondered what she was thinking.

"A midwestern girl."

"Something like that," she grinned. "Born and raised there, but since I have no family to go back to, I don't consider it home anymore."

"Home is where the heart is," I offered with a smirk.

She snorted an endearing laugh that drew my eyes to the bounce of her breasts and back up to the curve of her lips. "You are such a cheese monster."

"That's such a farm girl thing to say," I teased, laughing at her affronted look. I laughed even harder when she flipped me the bird.

CHAPTER 9
NINA

Enjoying a decadent lunch in the middle of a workday was nice, if a bit surreal for a girl who lives by meager means. I didn't have a damn thing going for me, other than a need to cook and a desire to be around actual human beings instead of holed up at Preston's place on the outskirts of town.

"You can go on and tuck that frown away, girly, because I ain't affected at all. Nope, not at all." Buddy stared back at me firmly, the air between us heavy with infinite stubbornness. "I'm sorry, Nina, but I can't risk having you fall on spilled beer or fried chicken grease and re-injure yourself. I won't have that on my conscience. When the doc says you're all clear, you can come back."

I let out a dramatic sigh, thick with frustration,

but nodded at Buddy's words. "I understand." And I really did, but that didn't mean I wasn't pissed.

Still, I knew arguing with Buddy would do nothing to get me back behind the bar. And I needed to get moving so I could pick up the groceries with this irritating boot making things way harder than they should be.

"Don't go and do nothing stupid now, Nina. I mean it. You're a part of Tulip, and folks will pitch in to help. I guarantee it."

There was a bookstore in town where I could grab a newspaper on the way home, to scope out the classifieds section. Until then, I would have to be frugal and push my savings as far as it could go. Since I couldn't drive with the boot, I'd save on gas, and since I couldn't cook to save my life, I'd also save on food.

"You want something to eat?" Buddy asks, well aware of my lack of kitchen skills.

"Nope. I have a few more stops to make, and I'd prefer to not lug around any extra pounds. Thanks." I watched Buddy turn away, grumbling under his breath, leaving me and the last of my beer in peace.

But it didn't last long — not the beer or the peace.

"You look like someone ripped out a piercing."

Jayne smiled at me, her green eyes shining and her dimples winking with joy.

"Gee, thanks," I grunted and rolled my eyes as I finished off my drink. "Good to see you, Jayne." Now was as good a time as any to get on with my errands.

"Oh, don't be so sensitive, Nina, I'm here to help. Honestly." Her smile brightened, making her look barely legal instead of the twenty-something I'd guessed she was. "Hey, Buddy, can I get a margarita?"

Buddy hated mixed drinks, and Jayne knew it. She winked at him, anticipating his regular complaints about how drinking should be done as the good lord intended — from a tap or in a glass. The end.

When her gaze swung back to me, I shrugged like it didn't matter even though it mattered more than I wanted it to. "Yeah? And who's benefitting from this help, me or someone else?"

Her laugh was good-natured as she gave my shoulder a playful bump. "I like you, Nina. You're always honest and you don't scare easily. Why does it have to be either or?" Her question was so abrupt that it nearly gave me whiplash. I knew she'd done it on purpose.

"In my experience, it usually is. I'm open to being surprised."

"And I love surprising people, so we're already a perfect match." Jayne tossed back the rest of her margarita and nodded toward the wall as she slid off the stool. "Hey Buddy, can you bring us a pitcher of margaritas and the overloaded nachos? Extra jalapeños. Come on," she called to me as she walked away, certain I would follow.

I would. Silently. In a quiet booth, we sat facing each other and saying nothing, both of us too stubborn to get on with it. At least, until Buddy set the pitcher and two chilled glasses between us. "I have a drink. Talk."

Her lips twitched in amusement. Most of the people here were too polite to speed her along, instead indulging her whims, tangents, and oversharing. "Were you around when the tornado hit?"

"No, I arrived in Tulip not long after. But I helped with the cleanup." It was probably why the good folks of Tulip hadn't judged me too harshly when they'd caught sight of my body modifications.

"Well, then, I'm sure you've heard all about Tulip's Tribute on the town square. The statue is cracked, the garden has been trampled, and the fountain needs to be restored." She sighed dramatically and rolled her eyes. "Of course, the Worthington family would love to just toss a few bucks at it and call all the shots, but the town wants to do it."

"Yeah, I've heard about it — it's the main topic of conversation just about everywhere you go. I really don't see what any of this has to do with me, but you can put me down to plant flowers or whatever when the time comes." A little bit of time and elbow grease went a long way in this town, and I had no problem doing my part.

"You're a big hero right now, and rightfully so," she added with another dimpled smile. "And we should capitalize on it. Strike while the iron is hot, and all that." It was starting to sound like there'd be some kind of angle, and I didn't like it. I didn't *do* angles. I did straightforward. Clear cut.

"Don't let my appearance fool you. I'm not a crook."

She looked genuinely offended. "I didn't think you were, but I really didn't think you were so prickly, either." Jayne held up a hand to stop the smart-ass remark perched on the tip of my tongue. "Listen. To raise money for the Tribute, we're putting together a 'Hometown Heroes' calendar of all the hunky men in town. Mostly the ones who work emergency jobs like police, fire, and EMT."

"And Search and Rescue," I added, one brow arched in suspicion.

"Yes. Look, I want this calendar to happen because I think it's a great way for everyone to pitch in using their talents — I'll take the photos, of course, but the town has already budgeted for a special events coordinator, which we haven't found yet." The woman didn't slow down, not even to take down a few gulps of margarita between run-on sentences. "And I can get you the gig."

I eyed that dimpled smile warily. I didn't trust it. When I told her as much, Janey only laughed. "What's the catch?"

"No catch," she purred, her lips around the rim of her glass.

"That's your first lie."

"How many do I get, exactly?" Her mouth twitched again, her green eyes glittering with humor. "Okay, fine. I need you to convince Preston to be one of the calendar boys."

"Oh, so, this isn't a real job." Because there was no way in hell Preston would agree. The man might have bucked his family's wishes for his career, but he was good and proper right down to his bones and I was pretty sure posing for a man-candy calendar was neither appropriate or acceptable, as far as he was concerned. "Got it. Thanks for the offer," I told her dryly.

"Look, I know it's a big ask, but I also know you

guys have been living together recently." She didn't seem to relish the gossip, which maybe pissed me off even more.

"We are not living together," I corrected. "He deemed my steps a hazard and took me to his place. He's high-handed and much stronger... you know what? It doesn't matter. I'm staying there temporarily, but I hold no sway over Preston. You'll have to find another coordinator."

"That's too bad. The job comes with a full salary, and would still allow you to work here once your leg is healed. If you want." Janey named an amount that was about what I hoped to clear with tips in a town this size — which meant it would double my current earnings. "Think about it."

"He won't agree." I didn't know him well, but I knew that much.

"It's up to you to persuade him." I was convinced Janey might be the devil, judging by her wicked laugh and suggestive eye movements.

"It's not like that," I protested.

"If you say so, though I don't know why. You're hot and he's hot," she said with a shrug, "could work."

"We're too different. Can you please stop saying that stuff so loud?"

"Why? Landing him would be a pretty big deal.

Not for me, of course, I've known him since before he was good-looking. I remember him with no front teeth, can't un-see that. Still, he's a good catch."

"You don't get it," I told her testily. "I'll try, but if I were you, I wouldn't stop looking to fill the position."

"You'll do it" she assured me, "and when you do, it'll make it so much easier for you to convince the other guys on my list. Call me if you have any questions. It would be better for all of us if you got that yes sooner rather than later."

She pushed her business card across the table as she slid out of the booth. "Talk soon. Enjoy the nachos."

I wished I had that kind of energy, especially lately.

"Hey Buddy," I called in the direction of the bar, "can you make those nachos to go?" He grumbled, but shouted the changed order status to the kitchen. "Thanks."

That would be at least two meals I didn't have to cook or buy. Maybe this would all work out.

Crazier things have happened.

CHAPTER 10
PRESTON

"You want me to do *what*?"

I was pretty sure I'd heard Nina incorrectly. We were practically strangers and, aside from a few looks I might have described as appreciative, she hadn't shown any interest in seeing me without a shirt. As soon as I set the pizza on a cooling rack, I turned to glare at her.

"You heard me, Preston. Don't make this more difficult than it already is." She was acting as though she were the one being asked to do something ridiculous.

"That's easy for you to say when you're not being asked to strip down and take photos for complete strangers to drool over!" Not that any of that sounded horrible but the last thing I was interested in was becoming higher profile than I already was in this town.

"First of all, don't act like you have a problem with women drooling over your hot body. Why the hell else do you keep in such good shape if you don't want women to appreciate it?"

My hot body?

"And I didn't say strip down, you freak. I said 'Hometown Heroes calendar,' not naked or half-naked booty modeling." Her sarcastic grunt was unbelievably sexy, but I knew she wouldn't appreciate that observation.

"Booty modeling?"

"Yeah, when you're selling that booty." She pouted her lips and stuck her butt out at an awkward angle, thanks to the boot. Still, it was adorable.

"I'm sorry, Nina. I'm not selling this booty." The last thing I needed was the grief that would surely come my way if my mother found out I was posing in a calendar. No, I was playing the long, stay-under-the-radar game. "Sorry."

She sighed and her shoulders fell, but she hid her vulnerability quickly. "So, you mean to tell me that a Worthington — the one who recently saved one of the Tulip's Troopers — won't do his part to help restore the Tribute? I guess I was wrong about you."

Her outburst felt incredibly manipulative, so I shrugged it off. "Maybe you were," I said coldly. "I'm sure it wasn't the first time."

Nina froze, and it was so slight and so fast I thought I'd imagined it. She said nothing in reply, just looked down at her lukewarm pizza and ate it. Reluctantly. "Not as good as your fancy pizza," she said, finally, "but this isn't terrible either."

It was food and I'd bought it on sale, which was often my only criteria at the grocery store — especially when I was cornered by a matchmaking mama. Which I always was at the market. "High praise."

She shrugged and turned back to her meal, finishing quickly enough to brush off any questions but without the gusto of someone truly enjoying her dinner. Nina hid her emotions well, but she'd probably be disappointed to realize just how much her face gave away. I couldn't take it anymore. "What's the big deal if I do this or not, Nina?"

She shrugged. "It's no big deal. You're not interested, and unlike the rest of the people in this town, I *can* take no for an answer." Her words were clear, and her demeanor was telling me to fuck off just as clearly. I couldn't figure out why.

Why should I be the sacrificial lamb for this calendar? And why in the hell did I feel bad about saying no to this completely unreasonable request? I certainly didn't want to draw a bigger target on my back, accepting dates with women I had no interest in simply because good manners said I had to but I couldn't help it — I hated the flare of disappointment in her sharp blue eyes and the way her shoulders slumped with defeat.

This was exactly why I kept my interactions with women simple and casual. I got enough drama in my professional life.

Nina could be as mad as she wanted. Tomorrow, I'd be starting another three-day shift and by the time I clocked out, she'd likely be well over whatever was pissing her off right now.

I hoped so, anyway.

∾

"I love it when the Potluck Patrol descends on the office." Nate grinned over at me, his mouth filled with their latest offering, courtesy of Edith 'Eddy' Henderson. "Can't say I've ever had meatloaf shepherd's pie, but it's damn good." He groaned again and it started to feel a little uncomfortable.

"It's all the butter in the mashed potatoes," I

informed him. It was Eddy's specialty, delicious and deadly. "Sure, it's good, but I can feel my arteries clogging every time I swallow. At least we have salad to balance it out."

Nate laughed, somehow shoveling food into his face like we hadn't already enjoyed two big breakfast burritos earlier that morning. He'd even had banana a couple hours ago. Three servings later, he finally came up for air. "They hit you up to do the calendar yet?"

"You, too?" I was relieved to hear I hadn't been targeted specifically for this project. Nina hadn't picked up any of my calls or returned any of my text messages so far today, which was fine with me. If she couldn't handle a little disagreement, we'd never really be friends, anyway — and that was all we could possibly be. "I'm not interested. Are you?"

"It's for a good cause, and I don't really mind if the ladies want to ogle this body; I work hard at it." He snorted. "Besides, it's much better than the Potluck Patrol drooling over me at the gym. *That* is the definition of uncomfortable." He shuddered dramatically and we both laughed. "It's too bad you're not interested, having a Worthington in the calendar might help with the fundraising goals."

Seems everyone was determined to manipulate me — or try to, at any rate. "Really, Nate? There are plenty of ways to raise money. If you don't believe me, just ask my mother." The woman could plan a fundraiser in her sleep and still ensure it was the hottest ticket in town.

"We both know if your mother writes a check, she'll run right over everyone else's wants. This way, everyone pitches in. So, how many calendars are you planning to buy?"

"I'll find a way to contribute." I always did, but rarely with money. "Did Nina ask you to talk to me?" Nate was touting the benefits of this calendar a little too much.

He frowned, looking over at me like I was the crazy one. "No. Why?"

I told Nate about Nina's request, and how she'd been freezing me out since I refused. "Now she's just outright ignoring me, like I didn't have every right to say no. What's that about?"

The more I thought about it, the angrier I got. Her behavior was childish. Selfish, really, when I was doing my best to help her.

"Oh, I heard Janey offered her a job coordinating the shoot," Nate explained, "but *only* if she was able to get you to do the calendar."

I couldn't help but stare at him for a long time, confused. "Since when do you gossip?"

"Since I was trapped in a booth with Janey while

she flirted and coerced me into agreeing to do the calendar." There were no signs of deception and more than that, I believed him.

"And that's true, about the job?" He nodded, and I felt sympathy welling up inside me with a lump in my throat. "Shit." A big dose of guilt followed. "Why wouldn't she tell me that?"

She could have tried to guilt me or threaten to use something. *Anything.* Instead, she had stayed silent.

"Doesn't strike me as the kind of girl to accept charity," Nate said simply.

"But Buddy isn't letting her work," I told him. "She could really use that job."

"Why do you care so much? She asked and you said no. Just be happy she didn't manipulate the situation, especially since you've moved her in with you."

"Come on, man. There was no way she could handle those stairs on her ankle."

Nate's look told me just how full of crap he thought I was. "And she doesn't have any friends in town?"

I sighed. "Max was busy with the after drama of the flood and I have lots of room – and no housemates. I told her to stay with me."

"So, it was all your idea?"

"Yeah," I admitted. "And she's been fighting me every damn day."

"Better than trying to get that wifey title, right? Or... do you want her to want that title?" His teasing tone pissed me off, but there was some truth to his words. When I said nothing, his eyes widened. "You like her."

"Shut up." I did like her, but it wasn't like what he was suggesting. She was funny and smart and, yeah, hot as hell, but we were just friends. Sort of. "I'm just trying to figure out what I did to piss her off."

"She's probably just worried about how she's gonna pay her bills."

Another stab of guilt tore through me. She'd rather struggle than ask me for help. "I really am a jerk."

"You're not so bad. A little stubborn and blind, but you're basically an alright guy." Nate stole another forkful from the casserole dish with a smile. "Just apologize, if you mean it. Or tell her why you don't want to do the calendar. Maybe she'll be reasonable."

Yeah. Or maybe she would be really, really angry.

CHAPTER 11
NINA

"Damn, Max, I don't know how you manage to make spiked lemonade taste so good. I'm in a special kind of heaven right now."

Leaning back in one of her plush blue kitchen chairs with my foot elevated on an empty chair, I closed my eyes with a sigh. "But I'm only staying until I can make it up my stairs without collapsing from fatigue. Or until the hoagies run out."

Max tossed her head back and laughed, a lively, feminine sound so unlike my own unsexy guffaw. "Stay as long as you need. I'm just sorry the upstairs bathroom flooded so the guest room is out of commission until then." With Max's guest room out of commission, I'd be spending the night on the couch. It wasn't ideal, but it gave me a chance to gather my strength and confidence before trying my steps again. "How are you feeling?"

"Now? Better." After leaving the Black Thumb to run my errands with a box of overloaded nachos trapped in a bag, I completely and totally overdid it. By the time I'd made it home with a few copies of my resume printed out, newspaper classifieds tucked under my arm, and two bags of groceries in one hand, I was a sweaty, exhausted mess. "Eventually, I won't feel any pain at all when I have to call you up just for help getting off my stairs. So embarrassing."

Max laughed harder. "What's a little humiliation between friends? I could tell you embarrassing stories about nearly everyone in town."

"I'm listening," I encouraged, leaning forward with my chin in my hands and a greedy smile on my face.

"I said *I could*, not that I would."

"Afraid they'd pay you back a little too much?"

Max nodded, tendrils of red hair falling gently out of the high ponytail she wore to keep the mass of waves out of her way. "They'd pay me back with interest, and some of those incidents I'd just as soon forget ever happened."

"Sounds interesting. Where I grew up, we were all too tough and too scared to be vulnerable enough to open ourselves up to public humiliation." My school experience was very different from Max's, which only highlighted why it was a good thing I left Preston's place.

"Sounds awful." Max winced and covered her mouth. "My god, Nina, I'm sorry. I didn't mean it like that."

"It was worse than awful," I agreed. "I'm sure your experiences were much more rewarding and educational than mine. Anyway, I'm fine, just worried." About my health and my finances, or lack of either.

"If you need me to float you a loan," she began, but I cut her off.

"I don't. I mean, thanks, but I do have some savings I can lean on for a while." A short while, admittedly, but I didn't want Max to concern herself with my problems when she had a little girl to raise and worry about. "I would just prefer to work, that's all."

After a few days of sitting on my ass, I already knew I would be bored out of my mind if I didn't have something to keep me occupied. "Enough about me, tell me about you. How's work and how is your secret admirer?"

"Still a secret." She sighed heavily and rolled her eyes. "Work is great — hectic, but great. I have a big catering job over at the Worthington place, one of those fancy affairs with six courses and more than a dozen different pieces of silverware."

Even through her clear frustration, Max could do nothing to hide how satisfied she was with her work. "Sabrina Worthington is a pain in the ass, but she pays well and when you do a good job, she's the best lip service around."

"Sounds like you love it."

"I do," she conceded. "No matter how angry or rude a client is, once they taste the food I'm serving to their guests, they're putty in my hands."

I'd never taken much time to consider what kind of job or career would fulfill me. The minute I'd turned eighteen — hell, even earlier — my life had just been about finding the means to support myself. And to be honest, that really hadn't changed.

"So," Max said, looking at me with interest, "are you going to see Preston again?"

"Not you too, Max." I groaned. Thanks to Preston's insistence I stay at his place, the whole town believed we were in some type of relationship. The evil-eyed stares I'd noticed from other women were probably the only reason I was happy not to be working right now, because I knew my tips would be for crap. "No. We were never seeing each other, he just bullied me into staying at his place using his muscles and cold hard logic."

Max leaned forward, a gleam in her eye. "Tell me more about those muscles."

I scoffed at her foolishness. "He's constantly picking me up and I don't like it." Even if I did like the feel of his muscles when he carried me, I'd never admit it out loud. "Anyway, I'm focused on finding a new line of work."

"You're just giving up? He gives you one lousy no and you're not gonna ask him again?"

"Nope. He's not interested, so I moved on. Besides, I think I have a line on becoming a virtual assistant. Doesn't require a lot of standing, and I can do it from the comfort of my home." It was by no means my dream job, but it was something I could do with this stupid boot and it would pay the bills.

"Oh crap, I forgot!" An alarm went off on Max's phone, and a frown spread across her face as she read the notification. "Callie has soccer practice tonight and I totally forgot."

She hopped up, rushed over to the fridge, and stuck her head inside. "I have to find snacks for after practice, but I'm pretty sure the last bag of oranges I bought is more mold than fruit."

"That's why I never buy fruit by the package."

Max emerged with a pineapple and some other

leftover fruit and dumped it all on the counter. "After the excitement of the camping trip, Callie needed comfort food and I indulged a little too much. She's not even sure if she likes soccer, but there's an adorable little boy on her team who is as big a dork as she is and they nerd out together. It's friggin' adorable!"

I frowned. Callie was just seven years old. "Isn't she a little young to be interested in boys?"

"Oh, it's harmless — this has nothing to do with gender. They both have big brains and bond over things other kids their age aren't interested in. It's healthy, and I'm encouraging the friendship because I'd rather she have someone she can talk to than force toxic boy-girl issues on her before they come naturally."

"You're a good mom, Max," I told her, admiringly. I'd known some truly awful foster mothers, so the compliment was genuine.

"Thanks." She smiled, proud and wistful, before fixing me with a meaningful look. "So, there's really nothing going on with you and Preston?"

Max's expression shifted from hopeful to sad as I replied, "Nope. Nothing at all, just a few days as housemates."

My words were punctuated by the sound of the doorbell ringing, and Max shrugged before turning to answer it. I leaned back to wait for her return — I didn't need to know who was there.

Max came back into the kitchen almost immediately, her arms folded and brows arched inquisitively. "Want to repeat that, Nina?"

"Repeat what?" She looked smug as she stepped back behind the counter, but before I could press her for more information, Preston appeared in the doorway. I groaned.

"We need to talk," he proclaimed. No smile or friendly greeting; just a barked-out order.

"Pretty sure we don't," I replied coolly, crossing my arms over my chest. There was nothing more to say.

"You left," he shot at me, accusation coloring his tone.

"I always *was* leaving, Preston — that's your home, not mine. And now, you have your bachelor pad to yourself. Again."

He looked angry, but I didn't intimidate easily. Not even in the face of a man with the body of a Greek god and the face of a dark angel. "Did I do or say anything to make you feel unwelcome, Nina?"

We both knew he'd been raised too well to ever do that. "No, of course not. But it was time for me to move on." *Before I overstayed my welcome*, I added in my head. I knew all the tricks people used to get rid of you when they were tired of having you around and I always made sure to leave before that time came.

"So you decided to trade my guest room for Max's?" His scowl and outraged tone were starting to piss me off. Who did he think he was, barking at me like I owed him something?

"Actually, it's my couch — my guest room is out of commission," Max offered with a smirk, and I stuck my tongue out at her.

"You're supposed to be *my* friend," I whined, feeling defeated.

"I am, sweetheart, but the truth is that between the business and Callie, I can't always be here for you. What if you need help and I'm not around?"

I understood what she was saying, but I was hurt, angry, and totally irrational. "I didn't realize I was such a burden," I snapped. "I've been taking care of myself for a long time without anyone's help and there's no need for that to change." It took me a few indignant tries, but I finally got to my feet and moved toward the door.

"Nina, wait. You're not a burden. I didn't say that." Max sounded annoyed but I didn't care, not when it took all of my energy and focus just to make it to the door without falling flat on my face. Or worse, my ass.

"Don't worry about it, Max. You're right, I wasn't thinking straight or I'd have never imposed on you. Thanks for your help," I shouted over my shoulder, grabbing my bag and stumbling out the front door.

Max and Preston called after me as I cautiously made my way down the steps, but the moment my feet hit the sidewalk, I was a woman on a mission — and that mission was getting myself home in one piece.

I knew it was stupid and childish to just run away. In the moment, though, it felt right. It reminded me of who I was, a woman who had mastered the art of leaning on no one. Living in Tulip had almost made me forget the most important thing I'd learned as a ward of the state: the only person you can rely on is yourself.

"Nina, come back!" Preston stubbornly followed me as I fled the awkward situation at my friend's house, and I forced myself to hobble a little faster down the road.

It wasn't a solid end game, but in that moment, it was all I had.

I'd only made it a few blocks before Preston pulled up along the curb in his Escalade, crawling slowly down the street next to me. "Stubborn woman, you do realize you left your things at Max's?" he asked me through the passenger side window.

Of course, I'd realized it, but pride dictated that my belongings were now lost forever — I certainly wouldn't be returning for them after my spectacular exit.

"I have my keys and my wallet, that's all that matters to me," I replied, refusing to look at him. Everything else could wait until I was more mobile or until Max took pity on me and returned it.

"They're in here with me." His words stopped me short and I nearly toppled over the uneven sidewalk. For just a second, I allowed my gaze to meet his, and I sucked in a barely audible breath before I resumed walking.

"Since you took it upon yourself to take them, I'm sure you won't have any problem leaving them on my side of the porch. Thanks." I turned right at the next corner, arms pumping with determination, as I heard Preston's vehicle stop and his door slam shut. I was about to whirl around to tell him off again when a big hand reached out and scooped me in the air. Ignoring my shriek of protest, Preston tossed me unceremoniously over his shoulder.

"Put me down, you damn ape!" I ignored the relief that shot all the way up to my hips at being off my feet and continued to pound my fists against his muscular back, his tight ass.

"Be careful with that leg, sweetheart." His words came out so calmly so casually, it was almost like he hadn't just lifted me up off the street like a sack of discarded clothes.

"Don't call me sweetheart," I cried, "and put me down!"

"Gladly." He lowered me gently to the passenger seat of his truck. "Happy?"

"No!" I retorted, sulking into the seat. "I'll be happy when you stop man-handling me. I am a *person*, not a piece of luggage you can pick up and put down as you see fit." Geez the man was infuriating as hell.

"Nina." His voice was soft. "Why is it so hard for you to just accept my help?"

God, there were so many reasons, but they were none of his business. "If I *needed* help, I would ask for it." And only if I truly needed it.

"Liar." He fastened the seatbelt around me, like that would stop me if I got the urge to run.

"What are you getting out of this, anyway? The whole town already loves you." *And the last thing I need is to be some rich dude's charity project*, I thought about adding.

"Because you need someone. You got hurt trying to save a kid, Nina. That was brave and stupid — mostly brave — and it's not right that it's now causing so many problems for you. Let me help you." Before I could respond, he slammed the door in my face and jogged around the front of the car.

The short drive to the duplex I rented went by in a tense sort of stillness that made everything worse. My pain throbbed just a little harder, and the silence seemed more oppressive than ever.

When the truck came to a stop, I slid down the too-tall seat and nearly face-planted. "Whoa, that was close," I muttered to myself, regaining my balance and continuing on the path to my place. It would take some effort to reach the top and I needed to prepare myself. I took a deep breath and turned back to Preston's car. "Thanks for the... ride."

A few feet behind me, Preston stood with a scowl on his face. "Will you feel better if you get hurt again? Because I'll let you, if it means you'll learn to accept some help!"

"And what happens when you have a date? Or a shift at work, or some Worthington event you can't get out of? Who am I supposed to rely on then? Myself, and that's who I'm relying on now."

He studied me for a long moment, his eyes focused like he was trying to figure me out. *Well, good luck*, I thought. I've got twenty-seven years on him and still haven't gotten myself figured out. "So, better not to rely on anyone, ever?"

I forced a smile. "You got it. Glad we cleared that up." Even the idea of the short seven steps up to the door sent beads of sweat dripping down my neck, but I sucked in a few more deep breaths and made it up to the porch with only a little panting. And swearing.

"You're pissed," Preston said, watching me from his truck. I tried not to look at him "I get it, Nina."

God, the way he said my name made it sound so exotic, I nearly forgot he was watching me struggle to do something I'd been doing with relative ease since I was three years old. "I'm not pissed, Preston, I just happen to have things on my mind that have nothing to do with you."

"Like money? You could have just told—"

"No, I couldn't have. I don't need you doing me any favors, and I really don't want to be your latest charity project, okay? You don't want to do the calendar; that's fine with me. End of story, okay? Good," I said without waiting for an answer. "Now, thanks again for the ride. I'll see you around."

I had something far more dangerous to focus on

— making it up nineteen steps with this boot on my leg. The first three steps were no problem at all, and I allowed myself a short break before battling through the next three. By the third set, I was drenched in sweat and about to collapse on the staircase. With an audience.

"I'm gonna wring your pretty little neck." With a low growl, Preston lifted me again, carried me up the final dozen stairs, and put me back down on my welcome mat. "Get off your feet while I grab the rest of your stuff."

If Preston thought I would just obey his orders, he obviously hadn't been paying attention. As soon as my door was open, I made a bee-line to the fridge and pulled out a beer to quench my thirst and cool my overheated body. "Exactly what I needed."

"I asked you to do one little thing and you couldn't even do that. What the hell, Nina?"

"First, if you had *asked*, I might have done it, but I don't respond to barked orders, Your Highness. Second, thank you for bringing up my stuff, but you can leave now."

"Who's going to take care of you?"

I folded my arms and fixed him with my best glare. "The same person who's been doing it my entire life, Preston — me. I'm not some damsel in distress; I don't need a big strong man to take care of me."

"It's not a question of how capable you are, Nina. Even the strongest of us needs help once in a while, and only dummies refuse to ask." He was right in my face, trying to get me to back down. Clearly, that meant I had to *double* down.

I pushed my face even closer to his, as much as my height deficit and the boot would allow. "I don't need help," I assured him. "I'm just fine on my own."

He growled again, but in the next moment, his big hands cupped my face. Before I could pull back, he pressed his mouth to mine in a searing kiss that took me by surprise and stole my breath.

Like the rest of him, his lips were firm and insistent, but instead of fighting the kiss like I'd fought him on everything else, I let myself fall into it. I leaned toward him and savored every second of his delicious taste, his tantalizing tongue, and the feel of his warm, strong hands around my jaw.

Then I realized what we were doing. I pulled back, wide-eyed and shocked, and pushed his chest back, hard. For a quick second, Preston looked confused, but he caught me when I lunged forward and our mouths met again. He kissed me until my mouth went dry, until my panties grew damp, and I clung to him like life support. It was a damn fine kiss

— the kind that led to other things, if a girl wasn't careful.

Except I wasn't careful. I hadn't counted on being drunk on Preston's kisses, on losing all sense of control at the way his hands stroked me gently while his mouth kept up an intense torture that made my whole body vibrate with a hungry kind of need.

As his mouth did wonderful, wicked things to my body, our clothes flew around the kitchen, our desperate hands grabbing and caressing each other inelegantly.

His eyes met mine, and our bodies slowly came together in a sweet, torturous agony that pulled a long moan from me.

He grinned. "You feel even better than I imagined."

"Right back atcha," I managed to pant out as he pushed in deep, pressing my back against the cold door of the fridge. "Preston." The moan was torn from me by his long, slow strokes that left me feeling lust-crazed. "Yes!"

With a satisfied smile on his face, Preston gripped my hips as he plunged into me, harder and faster, until my pulse kept time with the sound of our slick skin smacking together. "Oh fuck, Nina."

To see Preston, so handsome and proper, losing control like this, was my undoing.

He gripped me tighter and fiercely pounded into me until my pleasure overflowed as an orgasm washed over me. It was sharp and intense, sending shockwaves of electricity through every pore in my body. "Preston!" His name slid from my mouth in a slow, sensual rhythm as he pounded harder in search of his own orgasm. "Harder. Give it to me, Preston. Please!"

"Fuck," he roared, slamming into me. It was rough and unsophisticated, raw and unpolished. It struck me that the way he made love was the exact opposite of the way he lived his life in public.

He didn't fuck like the upstanding citizen he was, like the quintessential small-town boy next door. No, he made love like a man possessed. Like a man who indulged in the pleasures of life, no matter what simple minds considered right or wrong. "Oh fuck, Nina."

"That you did, and you did it spectacularly, Preston." My body was limp, sweaty, achy, and so satisfied I knew sleep wouldn't be far off.

He laughed and pressed his lips firmly to mine, kissing me as slowly and as sensually as I'd ever been kissed. It was such a stark contrast to the way he'd just pleased my body, and I closed my eyes against the way his tenderness affected me.

Because this wasn't about tenderness or affection, it was chemistry. A physical need had been satisfied. This was hormones and science — nothing more.

I pushed down the cozy post-sex glowing feelings and crossed my fingers, hoping that orgasm would give me more than just an incredible release. I needed clarity on my future.

CHAPTER 12

PRESTON

I can't believe I had sex with Nina, and I can't believe I'm thinking about doing it again.

Repeatedly.

The next time — because there had to be a next time — I would go slow, take my time and give her enough orgasms to keep that sexy grin on her face for days to come.

It was these incessant thoughts of Nina that kept me from having an effective workout. After thirty minutes of fighting with my distracted mind, I finally called it quits and left the gym.

Nina hadn't called or texted, and although her silence wasn't all that surprising, it still made me mad. Would it kill her to show her interest, just a little? Maybe it was ego, or maybe I had a lot more work to do when it came to her.

"Hey, Preston." The voice was unfamiliar and when I looked up, a petite blond stood in front of me, tits pushed out just far enough to draw my attention.

"Hey, uh..."

"Ginger," she filled in with a giggle. "What are you up to?"

I shrugged and looked down at my barely-used gym clothes. "Headed home."

"Want some company?"

Seriously? "Not right now. I'll see you later, Ms. Ginger." I sidestepped both her cleavage and the disappointed look in her eyes to make my escape.

But luck wasn't on my side — Max stood not ten feet away, anger flaring up around her as she glared at me in accusation. "What's the problem, Maxine?"

She bristled at my use of her full name. "No problem here, Preston, that's just your own guilty conscience. Or maybe it's your mind telling you something you're not ready to hear yet." She flashed a satisfied smile, arched a brow, and turned to walk away. "See you later, Worthington."

"Not if I see you first, Nash." She waved me off with a laugh and we went our separate ways into the small parking lot.

It was a small gym, too — most folks in Tulip got enough of a workout doing daily chores on their ranches and farms. But the town's little gym meant I could stop pretending to help out on Worthington Ranch on my days off, therefore limiting my chances of running into my mother. That alone was worth the cost of a year's membership.

Boredom set in about twenty minutes after my shower. Instead of being soothed by my afternoon beer overlooking the lake, I felt restless. And it was all Nina Ryland's fault. I couldn't stop thinking about her, worrying about her. Wondering what she was doing.

"May as well stop torturing myself," I announced determinedly. Before I changed from my gym shorts and into a pair of worn jeans, I placed a big order at Enzo's Fine Dining – who could say no to a delicious meal?

Since Enzo's was on the other side of town, I took the scenic route to pick up the food and parked my car behind Nina's in her wide, semi-paved driveway. Chances were, she wouldn't be happy to see me, but I was banking on her love of food to get me in the door.

I shot her a quick text to let her know I was coming before grabbing all three bags of food and jogging up the stairs to her apartment, a beaming smile on my face.

She pulled the door open and I sucked in a

breath at the sight of her. Nina wore a pair of tiny black shorts covered in light pink skulls and a matching tank top, which I expected. What I hadn't expected was what a turn-on the ink would be when combined with her pale skin and supple curves. "What are you doing here?"

I gave her an exaggerated pout. "Not happy to see me, sweetheart?"

I chucked her under the chin, which sparked a quick flash of rage she did an incredible job of extinguishing before she spoke again. "Don't answer a question with a question, Preston."

"I brought some food. Figured you might not make it out for groceries in the next couple days." I motioned to the bags, sporting my best Boy Scout grin, while she continued to glare at me.

"Thanks, I guess. Come on in." I saw the spark of appreciation in her gaze as it swept over me, and reveled in it as she turned her back to head back inside. "You have plans tonight? You smell good."

"Good of you to notice, darlin'."

Nina stopped just long enough to scowl at me over her shoulder before she limped down the hall, her boot making a loud *clunk* against the floor. "So annoying," she grumbled softly.

Somehow, Nina always made me laugh — even though it was usually at my own expense. Maybe I'd gotten too used to women chasing after me, or using nothing but my charm to win me a few nights and a good time. Nothing with Nina was easy, but it sure was fun. "How are you feeling today?"

She shrugged. "All right. The pain is mostly bearable right now. Why'd you bring me food?"

"So suspicious," I chided with a smile, which she returned. Reluctantly, I guessed. "Because I love the way you eat, *and* because I figured you might be hungry. Since you are the most stubborn woman in the world, I also know you didn't ask anyone to bring you any food."

"Maybe I planned to have something delivered later." I might have believed that if she didn't look so damned defiant.

"Bullshit," I pronounced confidently.

"Excuse me?" She tried her best to look offended, but I caught the glint of pride in her sky-blue eyes.

"You heard me. Bullshit. You were gonna go hungry or eat whatever scraps were in there before you left for that camping trip."

She looked at me for a long moment before dropping down on the sofa and elevating her foot. It had obviously become clear to her that I wasn't leaving anytime soon.

"That really doesn't answer my question. I've

been here for months, Preston, and other than your drink order, you haven't said a word to me. And now, all this. What gives?"

I had to admit, she was as dead-on right as she was stubborn as hell. "Maybe it's the 'don't fuck with me' vibes you give off. And on purpose, I might add." Nina knew she was intimidating, and she didn't do much to make a guy feel like his attention might be welcome.

"Either way, you didn't give a damn about my well-being before, and now you're acting like you're responsible for me."

"I'm just trying to help. Why is that so wrong?" I was starting to see why she hadn't made many friends in town – she could test the patience of a saint.

"Why? That's all I want to know, Preston; why do you even care?"

"I just do," I said simply. I didn't have the energy or the words to explain why I cared about her pain and her well-being, and I wouldn't until I was good and ready. "Now, can you bear to share a meal with me?"

The appreciation in her eyes turned to lust as her gaze swept over me again. "I'm sure I can manage you," she teased. "For a time."

I dropped down beside her and started pulling

metal and paper cartons from the bags. "Better make it a long time, or I'm eating both pieces of lasagna."

She growled. "You don't fight fair, Worthington." The little sneak took advantage of my laughter and snatched the lasagna from my grip. "Is that shrimp I smell?"

I held up another carton. "I had a feeling you were a scampi girl."

She burst out laughing, gripping the lasagna she'd scored as her body shook with the force of her amusement. "What the hell is a scampi girl?"

She couldn't stop laughing, and the sound was so incredible, I decided to wing it. "It seems simple, but its has intense flavor — kind of like you. Scampi Girl."

"Call me that again and you'll be wearing that second piece of lasagna." There was no fire fueling her glare, but I knew that didn't mean she wouldn't do it. I remained cautious. As always.

"How goes the job hunt?" If I hadn't been staring at her so intently, I might have missed the brief moment when she froze. She recovered quickly, though.

"It's going, I suppose. How goes searching and rescuing?"

"It goes, but it's pretty slow this week. Which is

a good thing, in my line of work. What do you do for fun, Nina?" It wasn't the smoothest conversation, but I'd never pretended to be smooth.

She blinked, like my question had caught her off-guard. "When I'm not working, I'm chilling at home. Watching TV, reading, dancing, pretending to learn how to cook. The usual. How about you?"

"Mostly I hang out with my friend Ry and his family, we watch a lot of football and hockey. I read. Grill. Drink beer. Sometimes, I like to get out to my family's ranch and let one of the horses stretch their legs." It wasn't the most exciting life, all laid out like that, but I had no complaints.

"A horse? Like, with a saddle and everything?"

"Is there another kind of horse that I don't know about?"

Nina nodded, looking smug. "A sex horse."

"Nope, don't wanna know. You ride horses? The animal variety, that is?"

She snorted and shook her head, chewing her scampi. "Not so many opportunities for horseback riding in the Missouri foster care system."

It was one of just a few breadcrumbs of her past that she'd let slip. I was like a starved man, hungry for more details, but I knew I couldn't push.

"I'll take you when your ankle heals," I said instead.

"Maybe." She hesitated. "Don't want my ankle to heal only to turn around and break a leg."

"We'll share a saddle the first time out." It would be safer, sure, and it would give me another chance to get my hands on her sexy little body. "That would be fun, don't you think?"

"I'll let you know if I don't get thrown or trampled to death." She went back to eating as though she hadn't just tossed out that bleak scenario.

"That's what I like about you, Nina. Your sunny outlook." She snorted a laugh that I shouldn't have found so adorable, and I knew I had to ask. "Is there a husband or a boyfriend somewhere?"

"A little late to be asking that question, don't you think? Or, what, you look at me and assume that I would have screwed you if I was in a relationship? Real nice, Worthington." The way she spat my name definitely wasn't a compliment.

"You didn't bring it up, so I figured I would." Maybe being honest would garner me a few points with her. I constantly felt like I needed them.

She set down the scampi and stole the lasagna right out of my hands. "You mean, you thought you'd find a way to bring it up without actually bringing it up, because that's easier than flat-out asking, right?"

Normally, that kind of directness would annoy

me, but Nina's candor turned me on. "That's another way to look at it, I suppose. If you're determined to be completely negative about it."

She waved her hands at me dismissively. "We had sex and it was nice. Good. It was really damn good, actually. But you're not looking for anything serious, blah, blah, blah. Let's keep it casual and see where it goes, blah, blah, blah. That about it?"

She was so smug, so sure she was right, but I desperately wanted her to be wrong. "Are *you* looking for something serious?"

"No. I'm looking to stay under the radar or, better yet, off the damn thing altogether. That would never happen with you."

For some reason, her statement offended me. "Because of my last name or my mother's not-so-subtle matchmaking attempts?"

"Both. And since the whole town knows that you don't *do* serious, there's no reason to go through hell for a few weeks of really good sex."

When she put it that way, what kind of asshole would pursue her?

"That was just our first time together, Nina. Imagine how good it could be, when I know what every little flutter means. Which moans mean 'give me more' and which ones mean you need it softer, slower. Faster. Harder." The pulse at the base of her throat fluttered wildly. She was turned on and I had no doubt if I touched her, her panties would be soaked.

"You have a very dirty mouth for such a golden boy." Her teasing tone made me hot. And hard.

I laughed. That was another thing I didn't do with women — laugh. Still, all I wanted to do was slide into her and make her moan. Cry out my name. "You have no idea how dirty. Go out with me, Nina."

"What?"

"You heard me, let's go out. Dinner and maybe a show."

She frowned, looking genuinely confused. "We're having dinner right now."

"Yes, but this is just us hanging out. I'm asking you out on a date. With me."

"Why?"

"Why not? We like each other and our chemistry is crazy. What are you afraid of?"

She barked out a laugh and handed the lasagna back to me, eyeing the tiramisu on the coffee table. "Nothing, I just told you my objections to seeing you." And the stubborn tilt of her head indicated she planned to stick to it.

"If you agree to one date, I'll agree to do the calendar." I always found that making sure both parties walked away satisfied was a good measure of success when it came to negotiations.

She crossed her arms and scowled at me, a look so black I felt my insides start to shrivel. "I'm not for sale, Preston."

"Good, because if I was gonna buy a woman, she'd be a lot less stubborn than you are. One date, Nina. Even if you decide not to go out with me again, I'll still do the calendar."

"We've already had sex, why do we need a date?"

"So we can get to know each other and have even better sex the second and third time. And the eighth and ninth, too." She grinned and it stole the breath from my lungs. "Yes or no, Nina?"

The minute she paused, I knew I had her. But a little bit of patience went a long way with her, so I waited calmly, arms crossed with an expectant look on my face.

She sighed and her clear blue eyes scanned my features, probably looking for signs of deception or malice. "Fine. Yes. One date, Preston. And do the calendar if you want to do it."

"You'll still go out with me?"

"One date." She held up her hand, in case I didn't get the message. "But I don't barter my time or my body."

"A bad girl with integrity. I might be in big trouble where you're concerned." I let out a loud whoop that startled her, but the soft smile she flashed sent a shiver through me that said the trouble had already begun.

And it was too late to run away.

CHAPTER 13
NINA

"Why did I agree to this? I don't have a damn thing to wear!" I opened the front door for Max, who eyed me with twitching lips.

"Aww, you're nervous. How cute. Lucky for you, I am a kickass friend and I brought a few dresses you can try." She gave me an assessing once-over and nodded. "We're about the same size, and your bigger boobs might even the height difference out a bit." She breezed in, carrying a garment bag in one hand and a paper bag in the other. "So... how nervous are you?"

I was nervous as hell, but I couldn't tell her that. "I'm a little nervous, but nothing I can't handle. Thanks for the dresses; I was seconds away from throwing on jeans and a pink tank top."

"You rock the jeans and tank look better than just about anyone I know, but tonight you might want to go a little more feminine."

I guffawed. "That's a sneaky way of saying I need to dress like a girl."

Max laughed, draping an arm around my shoulders. "You already dress like a girl — one with a great rack and incredible legs. Tonight, though, you want to dress like a woman."

She was right. I didn't want a total transformation, but I did want to look a different, hotter version of myself for tonight's date. "Okay, show me what you brought." I limped to the bedroom, anticipating three dresses I would never buy for myself and wouldn't dream of being able to pull off.

"We have your standard little black dress. It's great for any occasion, but it's pretty basic." Max held it out to me, and I took off my pajamas and slipped it over my head. It showed off a lot of leg, but she was right.

"It's kind of plain, right?"

Max groaned. "Apparently, I'll need to upgrade my LBD on the off-chance I get asked out on a date before this century is over. Try this one."

She held up a tiny red dress that was short and strapless. "No offense, but absolutely not. My tits will fall right out of this and into my soup."

She glared at me. "Do *not* order soup on a date. It's not sexy, trust me."

"Fine, I won't order soup, but I'm not wearing that red dress, either." Max was petite with soft curves that fit her body — she could pull it off, but on me, it would just look slutty. "Hand me the final contender, but I think I'll end up going with the little black dress."

"Don't be so sure, Nina. This one right here is pure magic." She held up a dress the color of wine, only deeper and more vibrant. "Take it."

I did. I couldn't help it. The color was hypnotic and the cut was short, barely skimming mid-thigh, but it was the long lace sleeves and exaggerated high-neck lace collar that drew me in. It was sexy, for sure, but when I tried it on, it didn't look right. "This is great, but it's not me."

"Wrong!" Max ignored the way I shrank back from her noisy proclamation. "This dress is totally you, Nina. Hot and sassy and super strong. Preston is gonna swallow his tongue, and then he's gonna swallow you whole. Just you wait!" The intense gleam in her eyes made me take a step back.

The dress was nice, but I had a feeling Max was doing that thing good friends did to pump up your lagging self-esteem. "What's his goal with this date, anyway? You know him; tell me the truth."

There had to be some bet out there, about him sleeping with the new girl, or something else that would make sense to me.

"Preston is a good guy, Nina. He hasn't settled down yet, but I think it's because he wants more than a merger marriage, which is what his mom has been pushing for. He isn't like his family. Preston will marry for love and she'll be a real woman, not a trophy wife. But... I don't think that's what worries you."

"Yeah? What's worrying me, then?" There were all kinds of alarm bells going off in my head, but I couldn't tell if it was because I hadn't dated in a long time or if I just didn't trust myself.

"You like him. You think you shouldn't, Lord knows why, but still, you like him." Her smile couldn't have been any more satisfied than if she'd been the proverbial cat with a bowl full of cream.

"What in the hell does *he* want with *me*?" That was the part that really made no sense. We had nothing in common, other than sexual chemistry. Why did he even want a date?

"You need to get over this whole 'I'm not worthy' thing, because it's getting old. You're awesome. Smart, beautiful, with a killer body and a sharp tongue. Preston is no dummy — that's why he wants you. And he probably wants to get in your pants."

"He's already been there, Max. I told him there was no need for a date when we'd already slept together!"

Max laughed for a good long time, smacking the wall beside her just to show off how funny she thought my life was. "Wait, you told him you just wanted to have sex and he's *still* taking you out?" I nodded, pleased to see she finally understood my confusion. "Wow. Maybe he likes you for more than that sexy booty."

I groaned. Those were the last words I wanted to hear. "I guess I need to start getting ready. He'll be here soon."

"Oh, I'll help." Max spent a few minutes setting up a spot on my tiny kitchen table, then parked me in a chair and began primping and fussing with my hair and makeup. "Preston is great, Nina. Don't worry."

"Then why haven't you dated him? And what the hell are we supposed to talk about?" The sum total of my dating experience was a quick trip to a local pizza or fast food joint, maybe a movie, but mostly, the bedroom. And even that hadn't happened all that much.

"Hobbies. Work. Travel. Your favorite sex positions. Talk about whatever you want, just relax and have fun. You already slept with him and lived with him — a meal should be easy." Max was right; at least, her words sounded truer than my lingering doubts.

"I guess we'll see, won't we?" When Max had finished her sorcery, I looked like a much sexier version of the woman I saw in the mirror each day. "Max, you're my fairy godmother."

"Excellent. I hope that means you'll listen to me when I tell you that panties don't go well with this dress."

"What?"

"Trust me, I wouldn't lead you astray." Max winked, slipping her shoes on at the door. "Have fun and don't do anything I wouldn't." How she managed to get the words out as she hauled ass out of my place, I don't know.

No panties. Could I do that, or would it send Preston the wrong message? Was there even a right message to send? I had no clue and I didn't want to start the date stressed, so I went to find myself some liquid courage. I needed to calm down — no good would come of letting Preston see how much he affected me.

When the bell finally rang, I took a deep breath and pulled the door open with a smile. "Damn, Preston, you clean up good." He wore black slacks and a blue shirt that made his eyes glitter like sapphires.

He laughed, and the adorable blush that stole up his cheeks only made him more attractive. As he looked at me, his gaze darkened, and the heat of it infused my skin. "I don't know if I'll be able to tear my eyes away or keep my hands off you tonight." He leaned in for a kiss and paused a breath away from my mouth. "Can I ruin your lipstick, Nina?"

Yes, please. "I don't know, can you?"

His laugh was deep and rumbling, his smile slow and seductive as he closed the space between us, spearing his fingers through my hair to bring us nearer until his mouth was on mine.

Holy hell, could the man kiss. His tongue slid back and forth along the seam of my mouth before slipping inside. The kiss was a simmering heat, just waiting to boil over — and damn, how I wanted it to boil over. Especially when he gripped my ass and brought me right up against that long, hard ridge of deliciousness.

Right where I wanted him, but with the added inconvenience of our clothes. Minutes later, Preston pulled back, a sleepy smile on his face.

"My lipstick feels ruined, is it ruined?"

He chuckled and pulled me in close, pressing a laughing kiss to my lips. "It's perfect. Let's go, before all my good plans go out the window and my evening boils down to being buried deep inside you."

"I'm okay with that."

"Nope, come on. The night is still young."

A shiver passed through me at the way he wrapped his around around mine, and gently pulled me out of my place. "Imagine what could happen if we stayed in...." After seeing the look on Preston's face when he saw me, I'd been grateful for Max's no panty advice, but now, with my thighs dampened, I secretly cursed her.

"You're a temptress, you know that?" His grin flashed, but he looked as confused by this *thing* between us as I felt.

"Me? I'm just me, Preston," I reminded him as we approached his vehicle. "So, let's go see what this whole date business is all about."

Maybe it was that panty-incinerating kiss, or maybe it was just being around Preston, but my nerves settled quickly and we enjoyed a companionable drive to the restaurant getting to know each other better.

"Are you ready for the best meal of your life?" He

parked the Escalade and looked over at me, his expression so serious that I reigned in my own excitement and nodded.

"That's a big promise," I informed him. "I hope I'm not disappointed."

Based on the smells wafting out from the building in front of us, I knew I wouldn't be disappointed, but riling Preston up was quickly becoming one of my favorite things.

He was a perfect gentleman, opening my car door and helping me out, and he even kept his hand on the small of my back as he guided us to the restaurant. It was a nice place, bistro style with dark wood tables and chairs, a black-and-white tiled floor, and jazzy French music playing softly in the background.

"It's great, isn't it?"

It was more than great. In fact, it was casual sophistication at its finest. But I'd never seen it before. "Where did you take me?"

"We're in Cheshire, about ten miles outside Tulip. There are no signs, and if we drive another five miles, we'll be in another town."

"So, is this your typical first date place?"

"What? No." He tried — and failed — to look affronted. "Okay, I found out about this place because of a first date. I kept the place but not the date."

"Okay." The restaurant had a cozy feel and a nice view of the stars blinking in the sky. After leading us to a private table, the waitress left us with small leather menus and ice water, and as I began reading the list of entrées, I suddenly felt inadequate. "What is a Cornish hen, exactly?"

Preston's smiled was gentle, helpful, and not at all mean-spirited. "It's a bird without enough meat on its bones."

I hadn't been expecting that for an answer, but it was enough. "What do you recommend?" Everything was expensive, labeled with foreign names that I barely understood. I was able to pick up enough to know it was all very fancy.

"Everything here is good. Fresh." Which was helpful, I supposed, but not exactly what I was looking for. "Just order what sounds good," he guided. "Unless you want me to order for you?"

I knew he was trying to get a rise out of me, but I felt too relaxed. And my body couldn't stop remembering that kiss. "Okay. And I'll order for you."

He blinked, but showed no other sign of hesitation. "Okay," he agreed. "No food allergies."

"Me either." And it became a game, each of us

trying to find the perfect dish for the other. "What's your favorite thing to eat?"

"Ever?"

"Of course, ever. I'm trying to win here, Preston; work with me." His laugh was full of life and delight, which drew a smile from me.

"Win what, exactly?"

"This dish game, whatever it is." It was hard to hold in my laughter, but I made a solid effort.

"Weirdo. My favorite dish is steak and potatoes."

Of course, it was. "Thanks," I commented dryly.

We placed our orders and spent the rest of the night flirting and laughing and talking. It was, without a doubt, the best date I had ever been on.

"I don't know how you got fish tacos from steak and potatoes, but I approve," Preston said, pushing his cleaned plate away.

"I figured when you ordered that second plate of tacos."

Watching Preston eat was hot enough to qualify as porn, the way he licked his fingers and groaned. The same way he had sex.

"They were really good." He flashed me a boyish grin and gulped down the rest of his lemonade.

"So, what you're saying is, I won?"

"Fine. If it means that much to you, then sure, you won. Dessert?"

Hell no. There was only one more thing I wanted in my mouth before the night ended. "Yes. But they don't have what I want on the menu."

"And that would be?"

"You." I fixed my eyes on him.

He swallowed dramatically and nodded slowly. "So, that's a no to dancing?"

"Just you, Preston."

"I was hoping that we could—"

"I'm not wearing any panties." That was enough for any red-blooded man to get the hint.

Preston shot out of his chair and threw some cash on the table before tugging me through the restaurant, practically tossing me inside the truck.

"Temptress," he growled as he leaned over, pulled the seat belt across my lap, then clicked it in as he devoured my mouth in a hungry-all-the-way-to-my-toes-scorch-my-skin kiss.

He tasted my mouth like I was a last meal he was savoring, sliding his hand up between my legs. I spread as wide as I could for him, and moaned when his middle finger grazed my slit.

He pulled away and looked me right in the eyes as he slid his thick finger in his mouth and sucked me off his finger. It was the hottest thing I had ever witnessed. I wanted that man, between my legs, inside me, right this minute.

He smiled, winked, and closed my door. Then, he quietly got in the truck, buckled up, and hit the gas, keeping up a steady one hundred miles per hour until we returned to Tulip.

CHAPTER 14
PRESTON

"No panties, huh?" It was all I could think about as I drove the longest ten miles of my life.

All night, Nina had been wearing *that* dress with nothing underneath. Nothing!

She shrugged, playful and gorgeous. "Who really knows, Preston?" She lay back on the sofa and crossed her good leg over the booted one. Teasing me. "Maybe we should forget this conversation."

"No way in hell, sweetheart." I kicked off my shoes and dropped down beside her, resting one hand on her thigh. "You're not wearing panties." My hand slid up her bare leg, stopping just before she singed my fingertips.

"No, I'm not. This dress wasn't conducive to any of the underwear I own, so I thought it best if I—"

Her words were cut off by a moan as my finger brushed the swollen lips of her sex. "Yes."

"Which is it, Nina? Yes?" My fingertip slid back and forth, pressing across her opening. "Or no?"

She gasped, nodding her head as her hips pushed forcefully against my hand. "Preston."

"So pretty when you're receiving pleasure." With her head tossed back against the pillow, her mouth slightly parted, and her eyes closed blissfully, it was the exact image that had been playing in my mind since the first time I'd slid inside her. "Open up for me, Nina."

She didn't even try to resist. Her knees fell open, offering me a peek at those plump pink lips. Her hair was well groomed into a neat little bush on top of her mound, leaving the rest bare. Slick and bare. "Preston, please."

Fuck me, I didn't think I'd like hearing her beg quite this much. "Please what, Nina? Tell me what you want."

Most women I'd slept with had been too timid, doing just enough to make sure I got off in hopes they'd score a Worthington heirloom on their left ring finger. I didn't want timid.

Light blue, almost clear eyes opened on me, and Nina's lips parted into a seductive smile. "What I want, Preston, if for you to taste me."

"Here?" I licked the seam on the left. "Or here?" And then the right.

"Right here." Two fingers walked down the center of her body, stopping right at the swollen nub at the apex of her thighs. "Never mind," she panted as her fingers began moving faster. "I'm good."

The hell she was. I buried my face between her legs, sucking her knuckles right along with her juicy, swollen clit. She was sweet with a hint of tanginess, hot and wet. And so responsive. I was pretty sure I was going to bust a load in my pants before I was even inside her.

"Yes, Preston. Fuck, yeah!" Her fingers tangled in my hair, tugging hard enough to sting a bit as her hips moved in small, rapid circles. "Yes!"

I smiled against her. Nina was as wild in bed as she looked, so willing to throw herself at the mercy of the gods of pleasure and soaking up every moment like it was her due. Her panting, along with the sound of my tongue sliding through her juices, turned me on more. "Nina," I moaned against her.

"Preston," she moaned back as her body began to pulse internally, her skin damp with sweat as goosebumps swept over her. "Preston."

I pulled back and, when she frowned at the separation, smiled up at her. "Make sure you scream my name really loud."

She glared at me, then kept her eyes on me as I plunged two fingers deep inside her and sucked her clit. Hard.

"Oh fuck, Preston!" Her body shook and convulsed and she held on to my hair for dear life, pulling it hard as she ground against me, riding out her orgasm on my tongue. "Yes!"

I continued licking her until she was a mess of damp flesh, wild hair, and a seductive smile. "That was music to my ears."

She laughed and crooked her finger to beckon me closer. "That was music to my body. There's just one problem," she said seriously.

"Oh yeah, what's that?" From where I sat, there was no problem.

"I haven't had *my* dessert yet." She licked her lips and pushed me off her, wincing a little as my fingers slipped from her body.

Nina straddled my hips and kissed me like she was searching for something, hot and intense like a fire poised to rage out of control. "Such a great kisser," she murmured when she pulled back.

"I see. All you need is a few orgasms before you start tossing out compliments left and right."

She chuckled again. "Maybe you're right. Best not let that little secret get out." Her husky laugh vibrated through my body, along with each kiss she placed on my chest, my abs, thighs, and even my sack.

I closed my eyes, letting the feel of her soft mouth, silky hair, and the scrape of her tongue hypnotize me. She gave every inch of my body thorough attention before her tongue finally swiped the length of my cock, deliberate and attentive.

"Nina." I groaned, as she kept up a slow and steady lick until my entire cock was wet and aching for her.

"Tell me how you like it." Her smile was devilish as she took me in slowly, eyes never leaving mine as I watched my cock disappear in her mouth.

My hips jerked when she swallowed around my tip. "Oh, fuck. Too much."

I gripped her hair tight and slid down her throat once. Twice. Three times before pulling her away. "More of that later; I need to see how wet you got from sucking me."

Before I could change our positions, Nina sat up so the ridge of my cock slid between her folds, soaking every inch of me. "So wet," I groaned.

She panted and licked her lips before she tossed her head back, enjoying the pleasure of sliding back and forth. "Preston."

"Yes, Nina."

Gripping the base of my cock, she slid all the

way down until we were fully connected. She stayed there for a long moment, not moving until she was good and ready. "So good. You feel so good."

I agreed with that sentiment — being buried in Nina and watching as she slowly came apart was one of the greatest experiences of my life. She took what she wanted, but not without giving me exactly what I needed.

It was wild, frantic, and intense as she rode me deeper. Faster and harder, until her skin smacked against mine. "Ohhhh."

She smiled. "Don't hold back, Preston."

The delighted laughter that broke free from her curled lips when I flipped our positions threatened to undo me. The sound vibrated against me and she didn't stop even when I gripped her hips hard enough to bruise.

Then, the laughter mingled with moans as I pounded hard and deep, holding nothing back and giving her exactly what she wanted. "Nina. Nina."

"Preston, I'm close."

"I know. I feel you. Come for me, Nina. Come all over my cock."

A little pinch of her nipples pushed her right over the edge into an orgasm so powerful it milked my own right from my body. "Yeah, baby. Let it all out."

I pounded into her orgasm, letting her squeeze me until I was bone dry, until my hips finally stopped moving and I nearly collapsed on top of her. "Holy shit, Preston. That was the best dessert I ever had."

I couldn't have agreed with her more. "Just think, we're only getting started."

Her bright laughter rang out again. "Just think, we could have been doing this all night long."

I fell beside her and pulled her close. "Just think, the night's still young and I'm off tomorrow."

After a short nap, I took her again — this time so slow she begged me to give it to her hard and fast.

By the time we were both spent, I had Nina half asleep in my arms, her soft curves snuggled up against me, and just one thought on my mind.

Right. It felt so right.

CHAPTER 15
NINA

I wasn't an office assistant kind of girl, period. I didn't have the sunny disposition that perky receptionists the world over possessed to greet hundreds, maybe thousands, of people every month. I had too many tattoos and not enough smiles, which made my new gig as a virtual assistant perfect.

All I had to do was answer a few phone calls, make changes to three different calendars, and take messages. It should be a fairly simple way to earn a few bucks — but I'd need to pick up a few office supplies.

The walk to Bo's General Store was long with my limp, but the weather was great: sunny and clear. I was smiling cheerful as I pushed through the store's front door.

"Hey, Nina!"

"Hey, Bo. How's it going?"

She shrugged, her face revealing the same wide smile she always wore. "Pretty good, but I guess I should be asking you that. How are you feeling?"

"I'll be better when I get home." Walking around town was great for my cardio but it made me a sweaty mess, which meant I'd have to struggle through a second shower once I made it back home. "Notebooks and pens?"

"I'll get them. Color preferences?"

"College-ruled. The rest is up to you." She smiled and bounced off, ponytail swinging behind her. "God, I'd kill for that energy right now."

"Nina! I don't know how you got Preston to agree, but you did. He did!" Janey squealed, quite possibly bursting my eardrum. "This is going to be amazing! You are amazing and everything is coming together perfectly."

I stood, waiting for Bo to return with my supplies, while Janey went off on a tangent, creating an itemized list of everything she needed to do, even though I was pretty sure it didn't require an audience.

"I had nothing to do with his decision." It felt true, and I *did* tell him to do whatever he wanted. Regardless of our date.

"Nonsense," she insisted, wrapping one of her arms around mine and giving me a half-hug before she took a step back and placed an envelope on the table with the words 'Benefits Package' typewritten on the front.

"We have a lot to do and not a lot of time to do it, so read that over tonight. And this," she added, pulling a green binder from her bag and slamming it down on the counter. On top of that, she placed an already filled-in calendar. "I'll be at your place tomorrow at nine with coffee and pastries. Thanks for this, Nina. It's going to be amazing!"

With that, she rushed out of Bo's as if she'd never even been there. "Did I hear Janey?" Bo called as she strode up with the items I'd requested.

I scanned the store. "How did you guess without any evidence of a whirlwind?"

Bo laughed and rang up the order, frowning when I held my phone against the screen to pay. "Before you moved to town, I was gonna get rid of that thing, but now it seems everybody uses it. Doesn't seem safe to me."

Her dislike of technology was no secret, and it always made me laugh. "I'll let you know when I get robbed, Bo."

"It's only a matter of time," she confirmed,

holding the door open so I could exit the store. "But I hope not, of course."

I grinned at her. "Enjoy your day, Bo."

"You too, Nina. Holler if you need anything else." I nodded and waved like I would do that, but I think we both knew it wasn't my thing.

The afternoon passed slow as hell. The three hours of virtual assistanting felt like nine hours, but knowing there would be $150 deposited into my account before the day was over helped.

The only thing that gave me any real relief was that envelope from Janey, staring at me. Taunting me. As soon as I was dressed for my appointment with Dr. Cahill, I opened the envelope and read while I waited for my Uber driver, Gary, to arrive.

The salary wasn't much, but if I kept my job with Buddy I'd be able to save plenty of money. The health and dental plan was what really appealed to me — I was sick of spending a week's worth of tips on insurance. It seemed like a good deal. Really good.

Almost *too* good, which was why I hadn't taken my name off the virtual assistant availability list. Yet. I had two choices: trust Janey and this envelope, or not.

A knock sounded on the door and, without

thinking, I pulled it open, expecting to see Gary's crop of blond curls. Instead, it was a petite older woman with a dark brown braid and jade green eyes. "You're not Gary."

She laughed and it was a good laugh, one that sounded like she used it often. "Nope. Betty Kemp." She held out her hand and I accepted it, shocked by how strong those delicate fingers were. "Ry's mother, and Preston's adopted mom. He's the one who asked me to pick you up for your appointment."

He did what? "I didn't even tell him I had an appointment." I was all set to be good and angry about this overreach but, dammit, it was kind of sweet.

"Sorry, thanks Betty. Come on in. Or should I call you Mrs. Kemp?" I never knew the rules about this kind of thing, but it *was* the south and formality was sometimes a sign of respect.

"Betty's fine. How's that ankle feeling?"

"Not terrible, but I wouldn't recommend this particular injury. Makes getting around a bitch."

Panicked, I'd worried I might have offended Betty, but she chuckled again. "I imagine it does. I broke my arm once, decades ago. Taking care of four rambunctious kids with one arm is not an experience I'd wish on anyone. Let's get a move on."

Betty was strong and capable, but I sensed she

didn't take crap from anyone. So I had no problem letting her help me down the stairs and into her little sedan.

"Thanks for this. I owe you."

"No, Preston owes me," Betty corrected. "But you must be pretty important for him to ask me for such a personal favor. He usually keeps his cards close to his chest when it comes to the fairer sex."

"We've sort of become friends."

That might be understating the relationship a little, but it was close enough to the truth.

"Yeah, well, all the single girls of Tulip are envious of your *friendship* with the most eligible bachelor in town."

That. Again. "Why is he the most eligible? Because of his name or his family's wealth? There are plenty of other hot bachelors in town. Believe me, it's now my job to track them down and get them to say yes to this calendar."

"Tough job." Betty snorted good-naturedly. "And you're gettin' paid? Sounds like you picked up a four-leaf clover."

"Did you forget about the sprained ankle?"

She scoffed and waved at me dismissively. "Wounds heal, but that's a good job. And, from what I hear, you've got Preston's attention."

"For now. I'm not holding my breath."

"Why not? I mean, it seems like you don't care about his name or his money — don't you like him?"

"What's not to like? He's handsome and kind and sweet, but he's also arrogant and bossy as hell." And I only liked the bossy thing when we were naked, which I was not going to confess to his best friend's mother. "We're too different, that's all."

"Ah, now you're just lying to yourself, honey."

"Excuse me?" Maybe I ought to reconsider the whole 'liking Betty' thing.

"You heard me. You like him, and the fact that I'm here means he likes you. But you're scared. A strong girl like you." She smacked her lips and gave me the kind of disappointed look I vaguely remembered seeing before my parents died. "Can't believe you'd rather stand with the hand you were dealt when you have the chance to get a few new cards and make something new."

Her bizarre metaphor kind of made sense to me, which should have been my first warning that I was out of my mind. "Should I be sounding alarms about your poker problem?"

Betty laughed, but would not be deterred. She pulled into one of the visitor parking spaces and turned off the engine before turning to me. "I'm serious. Don't look for reasons you can't be together;

if it's not meant to be, it won't." With those words, she got out of the car and marched around the front, determination written all over her face.

Her words echoed exactly what I was already worried about — letting Preston get close *and* falling for him, only to have him realize I wasn't what he wanted.

Or maybe Betty was right, and I was thinking about this all wrong.

~

"Give it to me straight, Doc."

Dr. Cahill had spent the past five minutes reading every word of my chart and staring at my ankle for so long I thought he was either making a move or having a stroke.

He smiled briefly before a scowl darkened his handsome features. "You've been overdoing it."

I shook my head and opened my mouth to deny the accusation with every fiber of my being, but he held up a hand and stopped me cold. "I'm not asking, Nina. I've seen you limping around town, carrying too much and doing too much walking. I can only imagine what you've been up to in private."

Embarrassment rushed over me, and I willed my

pale skin not to betray me in front of the already smirking doctor.

He was another one of those guys who was just too attractive for his own good, and a doctor to boot. Talk about unfair. Those dimples and black, Irish locks were model perfect—and I was struck with inspiration.

"How would you feel about being one the heroes in the Hometown Heroes calendar?"

It wasn't the most elegant of requests and my timing couldn't have been worse, but it's not like he would agree to a meeting with me since the whole town already knew what I was doing. Everywhere I went, people stopped me to extoll the virtues of this nephew or that grandson. It was annoying. And kind of sweet, I had to admit.

"No."

That was... unequivocal. "It's for a good cause."

"I know, and if you want me to pay for rental equipment or something, can do that. This? No."

Why were all the men in this town so stubborn? Most guys not even half as good looking would be flattered to be part of a calendar that women would pay for just to see them in various states of undress.

"If you're worried about it being tasteful, I'll tell Janey it's a condition of your participation. What's the problem?"

Dr. Cahill crossed his arms and morphed into the good-time guy I'd seen plenty of at the Black Thumb. "I don't want to pose for some calendar for women to drool over."

I laughed; it had to be a joke. "Newsflash, Derek, women drool over you anyway. Every single day and everywhere you go."

"Even you?"

"I don't drool, exactly, but I *do* appreciate pretty things."

He snorted a half-laugh and looked back down at the stack in his hands. "You need to do more physical therapy if you don't want to keep that thing on for another six weeks."

"Another six weeks, are you out of your mind?"

"Take it easy, Nina. That's an order." I nodded my agreement because, let's be honest, six more weeks of this freaking boot and I might opt for the perma-limp. "And I'll think about the other stuff."

"Seriously?"

"Yes. See you in two weeks, Nina."

"Or before, if we need to meet about the calendar," I said hopefully, as the door slowly closed behind him. I was optimistic — but now, it was time to brave Betty's blunt advice.

I took about a dozen deep breaths as the elevator

carried me to the lobby, and I limped out into the overly sunny day.

I didn't need to worry. Betty was nowhere to be found, and I didn't have her number. Which meant I was stranded, sort of. I had options, but they all meant waiting. I glanced around for a place to sit while I tried to work out how I'd get home.

"Looks like you could use a ride. And lunch."

Preston smiled at me from behind the steering wheel of his oversized car, which was idling next to the clinic's entrance.

"Are you offering both?" I called out.

"Whatever you want, Nina."

That boyish smile would be the death of me, but the way my name rolled off his tongue was an instant panty-wetter.

"That sounds promising." Unsexily, I limped my way over to the SUV and scrambled inside like a newborn colt. "But it can't be a long lunch. I still have ten months of men to nail down."

"Then we'll make it a working lunch. I'll give you the inside scoop on how to get each guy to say yes."

He was awfully cute, being all helpful and kind. It was something a girl could get used to.

A girl, but not me. "More first dates?" I groaned

exaggeratedly and he frowned, grabbing my thigh and squeezing until I laughed.

"Very funny."

"I thought so." We rode to Big Mama's Diner in a comfortable sort of quiet that was more than nice. It was easy. And a good way to lull a girl into a false sense of security, which Preston did as soon as we took our seats.

"So, Nina, what brought you to Tulip?"

I smiled. Every single person I'd come in contact with had asked the same question, so I told him the same story I told them.

"I threw a dart at the map and it landed on Tulip. Tulips are beautiful and strong, and it's been a long time since I lived in a small town."

Probably searching for a place that felt like the last time I'd had a home, I continued in my head. Figured that out on my own, without the help of a hundred-and-fifty-dollar-an-hour shrink, thank you very much.

"That's cute, but I don't think it's the whole answer. I look forward to getting it out of you." Even his flirty banter was adorable — and sexy as hell.

"There's that Worthington confidence I've been hearing so much about."

He flashed a mock frown. "Who's been talking?"

The question was, who hadn't been. Somehow,

word had gotten around that we were spending time together, and in addition to people stopping to tell me who should be in the calendar, they were now also stopping to tell stories of a young, cocky Preston, good at everything he did from debate club to quarterback. "Wouldn't you like to know?"

Something dirty was on the tip of his tongue, but the arrival of our server was a welcome relief. "What'll it be for our resident heroes?"

"I just corral the heroes," I assured her. "But I'll have the fried chicken and waffles, the spicy blend. And peach tea, thanks."

"Meatloaf. And those dill mashed potatoes sound amazing. With some corn on the cob, too." Preston flashed that Worthington smile and the server blushed down to her toes. "I'll have ice water to drink. Thanks."

"Where do you put it all?"

"I run five miles nearly every day, and when I work, we do plenty of circuits of our designated areas. Miles and miles of circuits." As he spoke, my mind wandered to images of him shirtless and sweaty, his golden chest heaving as he panted heavily. "I'd love to know where your mind went just now."

"I'm sure you would, but I was promised a working lunch."

He leaned forward with a laugh. "It's already happening."

I'd believe it when I saw it. "What's going on?"

He shrugged. "Mandatory training for three straight days."

I had to admit, it sounded terrible. "If it makes you feel better, I'll imagine you wearing very short shorts while you're traipsing through the wilderness."

His deep laugh burst out, sending goosebumps skittering across my skin. "Oddly, that does make me feel better, Nina."

"Good. I'm counting on those images getting me through my own boring weekend of scouting locations for the photo shoots. Got any ideas?"

A teasing grin played at the corners of his kissable mouth as he opened it to say something, before a shadow crossed the table. "Hey, love birds, what are we eating?" Ry slid in on my side of the booth and wrapped an arm around me, smiling wide with a gleam in his eyes.

"*We* are eating lunch," Preston told him, lowering his voice in mock irritation. "*You* are here for a moment."

Ry winked at me and turned to Preston with a frown. "You called and I came running, and this is the thanks I get? For shame, Preston."

"Cut the crap, Ry."

My side ached from laughing at their banter. I'd never seen two grown men so playful together. "Okay, boys, settle down. Ry, how would you feel about being one of Tulip's Hometown Heroes?"

"I'd love... to think about it," he said, mischief in his eyes. "But I want to be July, it's the hottest month. Or is it August?" His question was rhetorical. Preston and I sat back and enjoyed the show. "No, July. I want to be Mr. July."

"Janey will expect Mr. July to be shirtless," I clarified, "maybe on a gurney or something."

Ry threw his head back and laughed, not giving a hoot that all the eyeballs in the diner were on our table. "I like you, Nina. Maybe some of that sass will rub off on pretty-boy Preston. And I have no problem being shirtless for you and Janey. Just say the word."

I opened my mouth to thank him and Ry pointed at me. "My pants stay on."

"What the hell kind of calendar do you think this is gonna be?" Both men burst out laughing, sending all the eyes our way. Again.

"Just putting my limits in early," he said playfully, stroking his hair and pouting his lips like the perfect diva.

"I think November is still open," I teased.

Ry stood, pretending to be appalled. "And to think, I thought we were friends." With a wink, he rushed from the diner and caught up with a pretty blond with long legs standing outside.

"How are you two friends again?"

"A lifetime of mischief together," Preston said, grinning as he watched his friend walk away.

"Now that I believe," I told him with a smile. It quickly became a groan as my food was placed in front of me.

Preston leaned over the table with a sexy smile I could hardly resist. "Now that we've gotten some work out of the way, what do you say we get this food to go and head to my place to work up an appetite?"

It was the best offer I'd had all day. "Perhaps I could be persuaded."

A grin split his handsome face, blue eyes deep and intoxicating. "I'm happy to persuade you, Nina. Even if it takes all afternoon."

My hand flew in the air to call the waitress and ask her to box up our food. By the time she came back with our orders, Preston had my hand tucked in his as he tugged me out the door and back to his truck.

"Where's the fire?" I asked him sarcastically.

"All over," he responded with a raw honesty that

sent shivers down my spine and made heat spread through my body. As we drove the short distance to his place, the air was thick with tension and raw sexual need.

As it turns out, it did take all afternoon for him to convince me.

CHAPTER 16
PRESTON

The downside to my newly-revived social life was that I forgot to do normal, everyday things, like stock my kitchen. Empty cupboards were hard enough to deal with, but a lack of coffee filters was just un-fucking-bearable.

Walking a block from the street where I'd found a parking spot to Bo's General was worth it — she had good coffee, minimal gossip, and no chance of running into my mother's latest daughter-in-law-in-training, Cynthia St. James. The woman was a clone of my own mother, right down to the plain, boring-yet-tasteful bun she wore twisted her blond hair into each day.

It was disconcerting as hell.

It was not at all an option.

I pulled open the door to Bo's and froze, backtracking a few steps as my brain finally caught up to the image my eyes had just seen. A photo of me, at least three feet tall, smiling and wearing a plain white t-shirt emblazoned with the words 'Mr. January' in black block letters. I recognized the photo, but not the shirt.

"Janey, no doubt," I grumbled to myself, knowing Nina would have at least given me a heads up.

But I hadn't seen or heard from Nina since our afternoon before my training, which was nearly a week ago. An insecure man might think it had something to do with her enjoyment of our time together, but I knew that wasn't it. But it was something; she'd responded to my texts, but with a lot less sass than usual. I'd spent the training weekend worrying.

"You're in luck today, Worthington — I got hazelnut and I got a super-dark roast." Bo's husky voice sounded from behind the rack of potato chips before her head appeared, high brown ponytail leading the way.

"I'll try the super-dark roast. Maybe it'll teach me a lesson about slacking on grocery shopping." It probably wouldn't, but at least the coffee would give me enough energy to get through the minefield that grocery shopping had become, ever since my mother had decided she now gave a damn about my life.

"Somehow, I doubt it was laziness that made your shopping trip a little less desirable." Bo spoke like she knew something and though I knew she and Nina were friendly, I doubted Nina would have shared that much with her.

"You're right, it was too much to do and not enough hours to do it all," I told her honestly, but my words were met with an uninterested eyeroll.

"Mmmhmm," she grunted, filling up a large coffee cup. "Coffee cake? Muffin?"

"How about a dozen of those bourbon pecan donuts?" They smelled like heaven and would mean another two miles on my run each day, but I had no doubt they would be totally worth it.

"Go doctor your coffee, I got some fresh ones coming out now." I paid and Bo disappeared to the back of the store while I took a seat at the picnic table out front.

"Mr. January, you are making my life very difficult."

Dressed in his Tulip PD uniform, with his olive skin and dark hair and eyes, Antonio Vargas cut a pretty intimidating figure — but I was a hard man to intimidate. That, and it was hard to be intimidated by a guy when you've seen him drunk, heartbroken, and just broken.

"You must have me confused for someone else. I haven't seen you in weeks." A hard trick to perform in a town as small as Tulip, but somehow, we'd managed it.

He frowned. "Has it been that long? Really?"

"Yep. You were busy with that FBI training and then the task force. Have you even been in Tulip the past few weeks?"

Antonio had left Tulip for college like most of us, but he hadn't come home right away, taking a job instead in New Orleans and becoming a homicide detective. A few years ago, though, he'd moved back. He didn't say much about his time away.

"And somehow," he said, eyes narrowed, "you still managed to throw me under the bus?"

My lips twitched but I fought like hell to keep that smile from spreading. He was right, I had. Naked in bed, I'd given Nina the lowdown on how to get her first-choice heroes for the calendar. "What do you mean?"

"Don't give me that innocent shit, Worthington. Everyone knows you're sleeping with the bartender, and she was ready for every single one of my objections. Every one, Preston." Antonio's hazel eyes were hard, as usual, but the muscles in his face and his hands were relaxed. He was annoyed, but not pissed.

"Maybe she's just that good with people. Do you even know her?"

"Not as well as you do, clearly." We shared a laugh and he shook his head. "She wants me to be Mr. March and she won't let up — she showed up with bacon mac & cheese, Preston. I know she didn't make it, but I swear, it almost worked."

"Almost?" I couldn't believe he hadn't folded like a cheap suit. That heart attack on a plate was his only real indulgence.

"She ambushed me at work and there was no way in hell I would agree there. Gave me just enough time for my good sense to return." Antonio's voice was light with the relief he felt at the moment. "Why'd you do it?"

"Because a pretty girl asked me to." And because she hurt herself to save a kid when it wasn't her job, but that was no one's business but my own.

"So, it's more than a rumor, you and Nina?"

I nodded, feeling happy and smug even though I knew that response would likely get on Nina's nerves. "Yep. I think? She's tough to read. When we're together, she acts like she can't get enough of me, but other than a few texts, I haven't talked to her in days."

"Ah, the independent woman. I've heard rumors about them, but I've never seen one in the wild."

"I was wondering when cynical Antonio would show up." Whatever had happened in New Orleans had soured him on love in a major way, but I wouldn't bring it up until he did.

"You have to admit that she's not really your type, Preston." That much was true.

"That's because I was looking for one thing with those women."

"And you're not with her?"

Hell no, I wasn't. "Nope. I like her and we have fun together."

"She's been to your house," he said, knowing what a big deal that was.

"It was unintentional at first." But now, the more she came over, the more I wanted her to stay. Luckily, I was smart enough to know if I told her that now, Nina might pack up and leave as soon as the calendar was finished. "She's also worried."

"About what?" He snorted and I knew what he was thinking. What woman would have anything to worry about with me — or rather, with my wealth?

"About the mean girls who'll punish her out of jealousy, and the matchmaking mamas who want their daughters to end up with a Worthington. She thinks they'll stiff her on tips out of spite."

"And she wants you to make up the difference? If you want, I can run a background on her."

"Don't do that, Antonio. She hasn't asked for anything, other than to keep it lowkey to see if it goes anywhere." I laughed. "Can you believe she told me she wouldn't risk the tips if I just wanted to fuck her?"

Antonio blinked, then chuckled. "After spending ten minutes with her, I can, actually." He sighed. "I don't want to be stripped down to nothing but my shield, handcuffs, and hat for some damn photoshoot, Preston."

I laughed and covered my eyes. "Please, save me from that image!" His scowl darkened and I laughed even harder. "Just say no, Nina won't hold a grudge." At least, I didn't think she would.

"Maybe Nina won't, but Janey will. She'll probably follow me around town and photograph me doing the most embarrassing jobs just to humiliate me." We both scoffed, thinking about how many times she'd sought retaliation with her camera.

"Maybe you can get your Chief to chime in his two cents?"

Antonio stood and stared at me hard. "And risk him ordering me to do it? Hell no. I'll think about it." He threw a few bills on the table and shook his head. "Shift starts soon. Thanks for nothin', Worthington."

"Happy to oblige, Officer," I called out, with a laugh that only grew louder when he flashed his middle finger over his shoulder. If you couldn't abuse your friends, why have them?

～

Now that I had a regular visitor other than Ry, I figured today was as good a day as any to get my bookshelves finished and put up against the wall.

The weather was nice and I had a cooler beside me filled with beer, water, and sandwiches. I could work all afternoon, uninterrupted. Nina was busy getting the fundraising calendar off the ground, which meant I was on my own.

And I was fine with it. I usually spent most of my free time alone, unless Ry stopped by and forced me to interact with the world. But now that Nina was in my life, I missed her when she wasn't around. It was a little disconcerting. I let my thoughts drift to Nina while I sanded the inside of the shelves.

There were a lot of secrets hiding in the depths of those blue eyes, things she wasn't ready to share with me. Or anyone, I guessed. But I had the patience of a saint, and I had a feeling getting Nina to open up to me might just be worth it.

"This is what's kept you too busy to see our mother? Just buy some damn bookshelves."

My shoulders tensed at the sound of my brother's voice but since I hadn't asked him to stop by, I ignored him. These shelves weren't going to sand themselves. Grant groaned and I knew if I turned, he'd be smoothing a hand over his perfectly gelled hair because heaven forbid he actually mess it up.

"Preston, this is ridiculous."

"What's ridiculous is that you can't seem to take a hint," I retorted without looking up. My strokes grew harder; if I wasn't careful, this distraction would screw up my handiwork. I stopped and put down the sanding sheet before I turned to face Grant. "This isn't any of your goddamn business."

He snorted. "You're wrong about that."

I smiled. Without me, all the pressure and all the expectations that came with the Worthington name fell on Grant's shoulders. And as much as he pretended to hate it, we both knew he secretly loved it.

"No, I'm not. This is between me and our mother, so if this isn't a social call, you can leave." We stared at each other for a long time, matching blue eyes spitting flames back and forth.

"Mom isn't going to give up, you know."

I knew. "I don't expect her to, but I also don't care."

Sanding sheet back in hand, I went back to work on the second shelf. Mom could do what she wanted — she always did, anyway — but I wouldn't play any part in her machinations.

"Yeah, well, you should, Preston. Mom can be devious and underhanded when she wants something."

And I'd learned from the best. "So can I, Grant."

Unlike our mother, I didn't care about being humiliated in front of the townspeople, because I'd never held myself above them.

"She's our mother." Grant's tone was insistent and harsh, the same one that used to get me to fall in line back when he was twelve and I was his annoying eight-year-old kid brother.

"Then she should learn to act like it. She's the one who decided I was no longer a member of the family, not me. And as much as you pretend you don't like it, we both know you love it. Save the concerned older brother act and get the hell out of my sight."

"Goddammit, Preston." Ah, finally, his fingers dared to muss his pretentious hairstyle.

I stood slowly and walked over to him. A lot had

changed since were kids. I wasn't the small one anymore — he was.

"Don't ever come to my home, on my property, and think you can order me around. If you don't want to have a beer, or grab a sanding sheet and get to work, get the hell out of here."

"Pres—"

"Now, Grant. The next time I see you, it better be because you want to hang out or shoot the shit. If it's for any other reason, don't bother stopping. Don't speak and don't acknowledge me." I knew it was harsh, but this shit had gone on for too long.

"You don't mean that."

"I do. Mother did this to our relationship, not me. If you weren't so fucking blind, you'd see that, and maybe support me. Your brother. But, since you're incapable of doing that, fuck off. Please."

Grant wanted to say something more — I could tell by the determination in his eyes and the stubborn set of his shoulders — but I knew what he saw when he looked at me. A tall, angry figure, intimidating and ready to strike.

Finally, he nodded and turned, stepping gingerly over the sharp rocks and muddy divots in the road. My brother looked as out of place as could be in his three-piece suit and expensive loafers.

I resumed working on the bookshelves, seething

over his visit. Why couldn't things ever be easy when it came to the Worthington family?

The sound of boots crunching on gravel drew my attention and I stood, turning with a wide smile as I took in the sight before me.

Nina, looking good enough to eat in a pair of lopped-off denim shorts that still had plenty of fringe teasing her thighs, and a sinfully tight pink shirt that was a change of pace from her wardrobe's usual black, blue, and gray color scheme. "You're a sight for sore eyes."

She set her brown canvas bag down at her feet and crossed her arms. "Are your eyes sore, Preston?"

"Not anymore. All I can see now is you." It sounded like a line, the fact that she thought it did too only stung a little.

"Yeah? Well, you're looking pretty good, yourself. All sweaty and tanned." She licked her lips for emphasis, light blue eyes glittering with desire. "How's it going?" She nodded at the forgotten bookshelves beside me.

"Better now, but okay. You here to see me or is this calendar business?"

Nina gave me a slow, heated look that left my jeans feeling a bit tighter in the groin area. "Well, I *did* come for personal reasons, but now I have an idea of what your month should look like."

I groaned when she licked her lips, as though she couldn't wait to taste me, or was imagining how I'd taste, all sweaty like I was now.

I dropped the sander and closed the distance between us, cupping her face while she grabbed a fistful of my shirt and tugged me down. She needed a proper kiss. I put my mouth on hers and gave her the dirtiest, sexiest kiss I could.

She tasted sweet, like mint and some sort of berry. I couldn't get enough of it. Neither could Nina, if the way she was holding me close and slipping her tongue inside my mouth was any indication.

Eventually. she pulled back with a breathless smile. "What calendar?"

I smiled at her slightly hazy, sex-rumpled look and picked her up, tossing her over my shoulder because carrying her to bed meant I wouldn't have to wait.

I couldn't wait. I stripped her down and spent the rest of the afternoon — and well into the evening — kissing and tasting her, loving on her, and making her scream my name.

The sound of my name on her lips when she came apart was quickly becoming my very favorite sound.

CHAPTER 17
NINA

I'd never admit it to his face, but Buddy was right. There was no way in hell I'd be able to run the twenty-foot length of the bar, back and forth, for an entire shift, sometimes a shift and a half.

The past three hours had proven to me that despite all my protests to the contrary, this leg was slowing me down. Scouting different locations for Janey's photo shoots had taken a lot out of me, even though most of my time had been spent driving. Janey was a fan of outdoor shots, apparently, which meant lots of driving to the edge of town in *all* directions to see if this flower was in bloom or if the mountains were visible with the overcast. It sucked, but it was bearable. What wasn't bearable, though, were the long walks required to find her so-called perfect spot.

Unfortunately, they *were* breathtaking. And by the time I'd taken photo and video of each location, I was a tired, cranky, and sweaty mess — in no condition to go around approaching all the gorgeous heroes in town to ask them to participate in the calendar. Which was now at the top of my to-do list.

So far, only Preston and Ry had committed. Dr. Cahill and Officer Vargas were playing hard to get, so I still needed ten more hometown heroes to agree.

Since I was no longer presentable in public, I drove home, keeping my eyes peeled for the hawkeyed Dr. Cahill. He would kill me if he saw me driving, and it wouldn't matter one bit that I'd spent a full hour in physical therapy every day this week.

Safely parked in the driveway, I made my way up to my apartment, grinning that it had gotten easier to make the trip even with the boot. Still, I couldn't wait until I could toss the miserable thing in the trash.

I showered and washed my hair, ignoring the small twigs and leaves that swirled around my feet because I couldn't stop thinking about Preston. What in the hell was I doing, messing around with the town golden boy? One of the sons of the town's founding family?

It didn't mean much to me, but I was a quick study. It meant something to the people here, which probably meant I needed to back off.

And I would have, if I could have, Preston was too appealing. Too funny. Too sweet. Too sexy. I could admit, at least to myself, that I was addicted to Preston. Powerless to resist him.

So powerless that when he rang my bell a few minutes later, my feet began to move toward the door without regard for the long t-shirt and fuzzy socks I wore as pajamas. "Preston." My voice was breathy, giddy even. I was pathetic.

His deep blue gaze raked over my body, twice, before he licked his lips and spoke huskily. "Nina. I like you in pink."

I stepped back and pushed the door open to let Preston and his two giant paper bags inside. "Um, thanks?" I wouldn't even pretend that wasn't a weird compliment, but I also couldn't pretend I didn't like it.

"I hope you're hungry — I brought barbecue."

My stomach had already told me what was in the bag, but it probably wouldn't be very ladylike to identify the fries, slaw, and corn by smell alone. Would it?

"Nothing I love more than barbecue and true crime." The painkillers had already kicked in, but not enough to make me loopy — a fact I was grateful for at the moment, because I had plans.

"True crime?" He didn't sound horrified, which was a relief.

"Yep, I'm binge watching *Mindhunter*." Netflix was probably the most stable relationship I'd had in the past few years. Traveling with me wherever I went. Remembering my likes and dislikes. Even checking in on me. If Netflix looked anything like Preston, I'd be married by now.

"Do you ever watch anything happy or upbeat?"

Of course, he'd want to know that. "I enjoy the occasional comedy," I conceded. "But really, most true crime documentaries *are* happy stories because the good guys won, the victim got justice, and their families got closure. Can't ask for anything happier than that."

Movies that were packed with sappy, emotional stuff made me uncomfortable and cynical about their distinct lack of realism. Or logic.

"It's either *Mindhunter* or *Making a Murderer 2*," I offered. "The choice is yours."

"What's *Mindhunter* about?" he asked. I was a bit surprised; I'd expected him to argue.

He unpacked the containers from the barbecue

shop and listened carefully as I explained the premise of the series and grabbed us plates and silverware. "That sounds horrifying, but strangely intriguing."

"Exactly," I told him smugly.

Preston let out a bright, boyish laugh, but his expression quickly changed as he rounded the counter, trapping me between the sink and his big, hard body.

"Hey, Nina," he practically purred as his finger sifted through my hair gently before he gave it a sharp tug.

"Hey yourself," I shot back cheekily, but my voice was deep and husky. There was no mistaking what I was thinking or what I wanted.

When his mouth touched mine, the kiss began slow, languid. A lazy, sexy kiss between two people who had all the time in the world, a couple for whom nothing existed but our desire to taste one another.

Preston changed the tempo; sped up, his movements became short and jerky. His grip tightened in my hair and on my hip, his tongue plunged deeper into my mouth, and the hard ridge of his cock pressed into me, pulling out a long, anguished moan.

Preston tasted better than chocolate. Better than

pizza. Hell, he even tasted better than tequila. "Nina," he moaned when my hand slipped under the hem of his SAR t-shirt, exploring the impressively hard muscles covered by soft skin.

I wanted this man so much I could hardly breathe. I jumped into his arms, trusting him to catch me. My legs wrapped around his waist; we were fitted right where we belonged. I was hot and achy, he was hard and throbbing, and we both had on too many clothes.

"Preston, yes," I moaned in his ear as his hands slid down my back to squeeze and knead my ass. He gripped it tightly and pulled me closer against his erection until a whimper escaped my lips. "I want you, Preston."

He let out a strangled groan and spun us around until my butt landed on the cool kitchen counter. "I'm right here, Nina." One finger traced up the inside of my leg, from my knee up, but the tease stopped before he reached anywhere good.

"I need you. Now." It was an admission I didn't make easily, but with his hands making me feel so good and his sweet breath fanning over my overheated flesh, it was all too much.

My hands shot to his waistband, groaning at the row of buttons covering his cock. Still, I made quick work of freeing his erection, stroking it gently at first but then rougher. With darker intent.

"Nina," he groaned, and grabbed my wrist.

"Yes?" I could barely contain my smile. I didn't mind being playful during sex. Or foreplay.

"You're trying to kill me." I gave him my best innocent look and quickly lost myself in his eyes, barely noticing when he gripped my purple panties and tore them from my body. "But I won't go easy," he told me just before his two thick fingers sank into my body, stealing each of my senses along with my thoughts.

But not my voice. "Oh, yeah."

They plunged deep, over and over again, his thumb rubbing teasing circles around my clit. Not enough to make me come, but just enough to drive me crazy. And the sensation of him fucking me while I stroked his cock was so sensual, I grew frantic. "Preston."

"You're so wet, Nina. Is that for me?"

I smiled. "Do you want it?"

He nodded, his gaze heavy with desire. "I do."

"Show me." Something about being with Preston made me feel carefree and fun, and I loved it.

Slowly, he removed his fingers from my body, spreading them so I could just how wet and sticky I was. Then, he plunged both fingers into his mouth with a groan and smacked his lips.

"Change of plans, sweetheart." Before I could get any answers, Preston pushed me back and spread my legs wide so he could lick me, slowly and then faster, working hard to drive me out of my mind.

"Preston. Oh, yes, Preston!" My body began to shake, trembling as the orgasm worked its way from the center of my body and shot out through my extremities.

It was one of those out of body experiences, where I could feel myself looking down at both of us, leaving me stunned. The smile on my face was pure bliss and when Preston stood, kissing his way from my stomach to my mouth, the look in his eyes scared the hell out of me.

"That was fast." He laughed, but there was no mistaking the pride in his expression.

"You're that good with your sexy mouth. Now, let's see what you can do with that monster between your legs."

He laughed, again pulling me close. "You have a dirty mouth, Nina."

"You like my dirty mouth."

"I do," he groaned as the blunt head of his cock pushed into me slowly. He was long and thick, his rhythm slow and tantalizing. "But what I really love is the way you hug my cock."

The only thing I could feel was Preston. He was deep inside me, surrounding me. He was everywhere and it was overwhelming. My body was still sensitive from the first orgasm, but Preston was interested in my next one, sliding in and out of my body and pushing me that much closer.

My body was too sensitive and it was playing with my emotions, so I squeezed my eyes shut as Preston slammed into me, hard and fast, singularly focused on nothing but our mutual pleasure.

Although I'd been expecting it, the orgasm snuck up on me and shocked me with its intensity. Preston's was right there, too, and I felt every twitch and every jerk as his body shook with his pleasure, sending long spurts of his orgasm deep into my body.

It was magnificent. And I was terrified.

"I should bring barbecue more often," Preston said after we'd regained our voices, gifting me with a flirtatious smile.

"I don't think we're burning enough calories to eat like this on a regular basis."

He frowned at the unintended slight and lifted me from the counter with my legs still wrapped around him. "You know I have to prove you wrong now, don't you?" He smacked my ass for good measure, and I let out a laugh-squeal that might have embarrassed me, if I hadn't been having such a good time.

"I'm sure you do feel the need to prove me wrong," I replied smoothly, "but I feel the need for a shower."

"Mmm, I look forward to showing you my shower technique." His words were arrogant and hilarious, reminding me again of what a catch Preston really was.

"You have a shower *technique*?"

He nodded confidently as he followed me into the bathroom. "Yep. Wanna see?"

I slipped out of my oversized t-shirt and pulled off my sock before stepping inside the cool shower and turning on the water. "I do."

Turns out, Preston's shower game was just as impressive as his land game — but the addition of hot water, steam, and soap? Well, let's just say I might have developed a fondness for water sex.

"Goodness, woman, are you trying to starve me?" He patted his belly as we made our way back to the kitchen, where the food sat waiting for us.

"Nope. Just trying to keep you a little weak so I can take advantage of you later." My body tingled at the promise in his eyes. I wanted him again. Already.

But this time, I wanted to ride him and watch as he came apart.

"Food. I need food," he insisted, holding up a container of barbecue ribs between us.

"Come on. I'll even re-watch the first episode all over again. Just for you."

The scene was so domestic, I wouldn't have believed it if I hadn't seen it for myself. Preston sat beside me on the sofa, just a little too close, and we ate too much and watched too much television. And we stopped way too many times in an attempt to satisfy our need for each other.

Spoiler alert: the need hadn't been satisfied.

All day and night, that's what we did. When we woke up the next morning still wrapped up in each other, I hoped we could repeat yesterday all over again.

But we couldn't. "I have to work tonight," Preston said resignedly, pulling his arm out from underneath me and sliding out of bed. "Filling in for a SAR on maternity leave, effective immediately."

I nodded. "Alright," I replied, unsure of what I was supposed to say.

"Betty is having a barbecue this week, and we're invited."

"Um, okay?"

He smiled. "So, you want to go? Together?"

Hell no. "Sure. Why not?"

He grinned, kissing me one more time before rushing out the door. Seconds later, he popped back in the front door with a harried-looking smile. "After the barbecue, we're having a real date. Another one." His lips smashed against mine again and then he was gone. Again. For real this time.

And all I could do was look toward the sky and wait for the other shoe to drop.

CHAPTER 18
PRESTON

"Holy hell, woman, are you trying to make us late for the barbecue?" Nina opened the door looking hot as hell in a short denim skirt and a black tee that cupped her tits beautifully. And, because she was Nina, she sported one hot-pink Chuck Taylor sneaker — with her boot side-kick — to cap off the outfit. Proving once again she wasn't who anyone thought she was.

Her skin blushed prettily at the compliment and she swept her thick brown hair from her creamy shoulders. "I wasn't trying, but if you have some ideas about how we can kill an hour, I'm all ears."

The little tease knew exactly what she was doing. This time, though, I wouldn't be her accomplice. "We're going, sweetheart. Don't fight it."

She groaned and turned on her heel, shuffling

across to the living room to pick up the beer and chips she'd insisted on bringing as her contribution. "This is new to me, Preston. I know I hide it well with my sunny personality, but I'm not exactly a meet-the-parents type of girl. They may not be your biological family," she emphasized to cut me off, "but they are who you chose, which makes them more important. Even I know that."

There was so much to unpack in that one little statement, I didn't even know where to begin. She had a head start on me going down the stairs, which forced me to wait as she struggled with the boot.

"That's just dumb," I said — rather stupidly, I realized in hindsight. "Betty already loves you and if he could, Ry would steal you from me."

"Would he, now?" she asked teasingly, laughing when I glared at her.

"Gina, Monica, and Lisbeth will love you, too, and so will Monica's husband, Charlie." They would like her because I did, at first, but once they got to know her, I knew they would appreciate Nina for who she was.

"And it's not dumb, it's a valid concern. I've never done this before, and now, I'm doing it in a small town where everyone is watching." Her tone revealed barely a trace of anger or nerves, which told me just how nervous she really was.

"I'm sorry, Nina. It's not stupid, I just don't get it. You're incredible. Smart and sassy, sexy, funny, and just a little bit scary. What's not to love?"

She sighed as the car came to a stop in front of the Kemp family home and turned to me. "I'll be fine." It sounded like she was trying to convince herself more than me.

"See that tree right there? Well, that stump?" she nodded. "Mr. Kemp cut it down when we were twelve, after Ry fell one too many times."

She sucked in a breath. "How many times did he fall?"

"Too many to count. At first, we were seeing if we could jump and land on our feet, and then we wanted to fly like Superman. Can we add stuff to our bodyweight to fall faster?"

"You two were a terror!" Her laugh was husky and deep, sexy and contagious. "Impressive you both made it to adulthood and didn't go into Hollywood stunt work." We shared another laugh and she dropped a hand on my thigh. "Thanks for the distraction. I think I'm ready."

"You sure?" Her eyes didn't look certain, but she nodded and when I leaned in, Nina wrapped her arms around me and accepted my kiss. "I'm sure enough for both of us. You won't need it, but I'll protect you."

"My hometown hero," she snickered and when I shot a glare at her, she only laughed even more.

"Keep that up and you'll be walking home." Still, the threat didn't stop her laughter. The only thing that did was the sight of the entire Kemp family as we rounded the corner to the back yard.

"This is just the immediate family?" she whispered to me.

I went through introductions and Nina was a champ, enduring overly friendly hugs, cheek kisses, and compliments on her appearance. "Let her breathe, guys."

"She's fine," Betty insisted, wrapping an arm around Nina and pulling her into the house, with a wink for me.

"Don't worry man, your girl is fine." Ry handed me a beer and flung an arm around my shoulder. "They're just curious; you never bring women to family gatherings."

"She was nervous about this, worried you guys wouldn't like her."

Ry frowned. "She's great, what's not to like?"

I smiled and thanked the universe once again for putting Ry in my life. "That's what I told her, but you know women. Even straightforward ones like Nina can be mysterious."

"That's a good sign," Charlie pointed out,

accepting a beer from Ry. Charlie was married to my oldest sister, Monica. "When she's nervous or worried or just plain acting crazy, that means its serious."

I listened intently. Any man who could make my bossy, oldest sister smile for more than a decade was worth paying attention to. "Really?'

Charlie nodded with a wise smile as he sipped his beer. "Really."

It felt like forever before Betty and the Kemp sisters emerged from the house with Nina in the middle of the group, looking protected. "You okay," I mouthed to her when our eyes locked.

Nina nodded with a smile as she made her way over to me. "All good. I survived the interrogation and now I've been promised beer."

"With a shot of tequila," Charlie offered with a conspiratorial grin.

"Damn straight. I'm Nina." She held out her hand confidently and Charlie accepted it with a friendly smile.

"Charlie, Monica's husband. From one non-Kemp to another, welcome. I don't know about you, but I had two shots after my interrogation."

She nodded and nudged her glass toward the middle of the table, making Charlie and Ry smile.

Nina took a long sip from the icy beer and sighed. "What a nice day for a barbecue."

"You're incredible, you know that?"

She grinned. "They're nice. It was just... overwhelming, because I don't have any family." Another little nugget of information about the mysterious Nina.

"I've known them my whole life and they overwhelm me all the time," I assured her.

"Somehow, I doubt that. They love you, and I respect that."

It was an odd choice of words, but I let it go, filing it away for a later date. For now, I put my arm around Nina and enjoyed being around the people who mattered most to me.

Nina included.

Maybe Nina especially.

CHAPTER 19
NINA

"We need to make some time to go shopping. Together." Maxine's hands were on her hips as she fixed me with a look, several dresses draped over her arm.

"But I hate shopping," I whined and stepped back from the door so she could enter my apartment. "Besides, when will I need clothes like this again? It would be pointless to spend money on clothes that I won't wear."

"Women do it all over the world — you wear it again when your man has forgotten all about it." She rolled her eyes, like my concerns were completely unreasonable. "I don't mind loaning you an outfit again, but maybe you'd feel better if you had clothes that were more your style."

"Dresses aren't my style. Period."

"Why the hell not? You've got great legs. You don't have to wear heels if you don't want to, but guys love legs. Show' em off, honey!" Max was a force of nature. If I let her have her way, I'd be greeting Preston in pasties and a thong. "Do you have any idea where you're going?"

"Nope. Preston only said to dress nice." I was tempted to wear a pair of nice jeans and a non-graphic tee, but I knew what kind of world Preston had come from and I knew what *he* meant when he said nice. "Do you have anything nice?"

Max frowned, looking affronted. "All of my things are nice, I'll have you know," she informed me haughtily, unzipping her garment bag with a flourish. "Feast your eyes on this lovely rainbow of fabrics, cuts, and styles."

I took my time picking through the dresses. I wasn't sure what to choose. They all looked nice to me, and if I were alone in my apartment, I would have chosen one of the simple black dresses. But Max was giving me that look that said, "Go on and live a little. Have a little adventure."

"How about this one?" Long, red, and velvet sounded like a tacky combination, but the dress was beautiful. Sexy. Classy. It was floor length with full sleeves, but a split up the leg and a lowcut neckline gave it the sexy appeal that would drive Preston crazy.

Max squealed, danced, and spun in a circle like an excited puppy. "I was hoping you'd choose that one. It's gonna look crazy hot on you, Nina. Trust me." I did trust her, so I didn't pull back when she grabbed both me and the dress and pushed us into my room. "Try this on."

I almost didn't catch the dress when she quickly tossed it at me before getting to work rifling through my things — first my closet and then my dresser. "What do you think you're doing?"

Max popped her head out of the closet, with mussed hair and one sparkly red strappy shoe in her hand. "Sweet baby jesus, I'm so glad you have red shoes! You only need one, the boot will add enough height, and he won't even see it. Now, let's figure out your lingerie situation."

"Your last situation ended pretty well for both of us, so that's an option." She glared sarcastically at me, and I laughed. "Just saying."

"This is velvet, Nina. It requires a delicate touch, not a tomahawk." I don't know how she was able to spend that much time in my underwear drawer, since it wasn't like I had all that many. "Here we go," she announced proudly, and I laughed again.

"It took you five minutes to find a tiny, red velvet thong?"

She shrugged. "I found the green one first, but I figured you'd want to match if you planned on gettin' busy tonight." Max gyrated her hips and hummed some sexy times music and all I could do was keep laughing.

"Sexy is great, Max, but honestly, I'd settle for not making a fool of myself. I still don't know where we're going, and I'm terrified he'll take me to a country club or some place where I am guaranteed to stick out like a sore thumb." Max's eyes went wide with shock. "What?"

"I've never seen you scared before," she admitted.

"Yeah, well, maybe if I exercised a bit more brainpower, I wouldn't be limping around town on a bum leg." I wasn't scared. I was nervous.

"Preston isn't a jerk. If he takes you somewhere nice, it's because he thinks you'll like it. Or because he wants to share something special with you. Don't overthink this so much, just have fun."

"Easy for you to say."

"Excuse me?" Hand back on her hip, Max looked every inch the hard-assed, super-capable single mom she was. "I'd love it if some really great guy became fascinated with me and wanted to share special things with me."

Okay, I sounded like a jerk. "I'm sorry, but this is new for me." I paused and looked at Max— the first woman who'd befriended me in this town, and I still treated her like I treated everyone else. "I've never done this before, Max. The few dates I've been on have been, let's just say, immature. Pizza shops and cheap restaurants. Mostly chillin' and then sex."

"Seriously? What about in high school?"

I shrugged. "My parents died when I was young and my Uncle Rudy took me in when I was seven. We looked after each other; it was just him and me, and that was all I needed. He died when I was fifteen, and any hope I had of a normal childhood flew out the window."

"Aw, Nina. No wonder you're so independent and strong." She flashed a grin that was more sympathy than pity and *that*, I could live with. "You can do this. Preston is a great guy and he's easy to be around. Follow his lead and if you feel weird, tell him."

That sounded a lot easier as advice than I was sure it would in deed. "I've already agreed to the date, so all I can do now is get through it."

"No! All you can do is have fun. Have. Fun. That's

an order!" Max had her sassy mama features back on, so I nodded and gave her a polite smile.

"Yes, Ma'am."

She smiled. "That's better. Now, go put on those invisible panties so we can do your hair and makeup."

I laughed when she smacked my butt, feeling light and free. For once, I actually felt like I belonged, and I knew I owed it to Max. "Thank you, Max. For being my friend and for being easy to like."

She winked, her grin growing bigger by the second. "Anytime, honey. And thanks for showing my little girl that women are heroes, too."

God, that just warmed my heart. I shook my head to get rid of those soft, teary feelings.

"She's the coolest kid I know and hanging with her is no hardship."

Max laughed. "Let's see if you'll be saying that when you have sex on tap."

"Hey," I frowned. "Hoes before bros, right?"

Max shot me a funny look, laughed, and shook her head. "Did you just call my kid a—"

"Oops!" I smacked a hand over my mouth. "That's not what I meant. You know what I mean."

She did an admirable job keeping the giggles at bay for a few moments, but they eventually broke free, loud and full of joy. "That was priceless." She laughed some more before regaining her composure. "I fully subscribe to hoes before bros, Nina."

Thank goodness for that.

"Now, quit messin' around. We've got to get you ready for this date."

I had a feeling I was as ready as I would ever be.

~

"You look fantastic, Nina." Preston stared at me with a goofy smile that made me feel sexy and confident, not to mention happy with my dress choice.

"You said that already." He'd said it at least half a dozen times since he'd picked me up, but it was the way his gaze kept sliding to me while he drove that had my thighs clenched tight and an unstoppable grin on my face. "Not that I mind hearing it, but you did say it. A lot."

"Who knew velvet was your fabric?" He tapped his fingers on the steering wheel as though it were the only thing keeping his hands from ravishing me. "Honestly, it's taking all the energy and willpower I have not to turn this car around and spend the rest of the week buried inside you."

I swallowed hard. "You know my feelings on that idea."

Preston smirked. "We're having this date, Nina. No matter how much you tempt me."

It was a nice sentiment, even if I didn't totally understand it. I mean, I was a sure thing and he *still* wanted to take me on a date? What the hell was up with that? But it was kind of nice, so I sat in the passenger seat and tried to find some excitement about wherever he was taking me. Since he was wearing a suit — a gorgeous dark blue number that made his eyes glitter like jewels — I knew we were going somewhere super fancy.

"We're here."

I couldn't say exactly what about the building in front of us sent me into freak out mode, but it totally and completely did. Maybe it was the name, Blackstone. Just one word, with no indication of the cuisine served inside or even *if* food was served at all. "Um, okay."

Preston was the perfect gentleman, escorting me from the car with his hand pressed to my lower back, and pulling open the door once we reached the restaurant.

We were shown to a large, dark wood table covered with enough dishes to feed six people — but apparently, they were all for the two of us. Preston pulled out my chair and guided me into my seat. And then, there was the hostess, with her model-perfect hair and body and billboard-bright smile. "Enjoy your meal," she said sweetly and, I kid you not, did a little bow.

A fucking bow. "This place is kind of... a lot, isn't it?"

Preston flashed a knowing smile. "It's well past 'a lot' and right into 'over the top,' but let's see how you feel after you've tasted the best steak you will ever put in your mouth."

His words, and the jovial way he said them, made me feel a little better about this place, but I couldn't tamp down my nerves no matter how hard I tried. "Steak is the magic word, Mister."

There was that boyish grin again. "I thought it might be." A waitress stopped at our table — another model in training, I assumed — to take our orders. She showed off her tits and smiled at Preston, all while somehow ignoring me.

"Is that everything?" she asked after he'd given her his drink order.

"Since there's another person at the table, that seems unlikely, doesn't it?" What can I say, when I felt nervous or threatened, my bitch factor increased by a power of ten. Or something like that. At least she had the decency to look embarrassed, but I wasn't buying it. "Irish Whiskey, rocks."

She stared at me and I stared at her, daring her

to piss me off so I could unleash my nerves and unease on her. But all I got was a polite, short nod as she flounced off.

"So, Nina." I held my breath, certain he had something to say about how I'd just spoken to our waitress, but once again, Preston surprised me. "Tell me about yourself."

"Not much to tell," I admitted. "I grew up in a small town outside St. Louis with my Uncle Rudy, who raised me. At least, until he died."

"I'm sorry, Nina." Preston's face actually looked genuinely sorry.

Still, I shrugged the same way I always did. "It still hurts. Rudy was great, gave up his bachelor lifestyle to raise me." Some days, I wondered if the stress of raising a kid he hadn't planned on had killed him prematurely. I tried not to think about it too hard.

"Your parents?"

"Died when I was seven." If ever there was a sign that people shouldn't get too close to me, there it was. "I have no other family, at least that I know of. So, see? Nothing to tell."

Preston smiled and leaned forward. "But that's where you're wrong, Nina. I've learned so much about you just now." His words were flirty, and his deep blue eyes held a promise I hoped he intended to keep. For tonight, anyway.

The waitress returned with our drinks and a platter of mostly unidentifiable foods. My heart sank. "What is that?"

Preston's smile was wide and amused, but not mean-spirited. "Those are oysters. They don't look like much, but some people like them."

"Do you? Because I might have to seriously reconsider our good night kiss."

"Then maybe we should get it out of the way now," he drawled and leaned further across the table. His smile was far too sexy.

"Maybe we should," I agreed and shifted toward him, waiting for his lips to come in contact with mine. When they did, my whole body sighed and relaxed into him. Preston's kisses were like heaven, wrapped up in chocolate and lobster, and I didn't want it to end.

But it seemed someone else had other ideas. The sound of a throat clearing pulled us apart, slowly, but Preston's slow smile kept my blood simmering.

"Really, Preston, what a horrid public display!"

It had been years since I'd had real mom or even a maternal figure in my life, but that tone of disappointment had "mom" written all over it. His jaw tensed as his gaze took in the two icy blonds, one with blue eyes just like Preston's and the other with pale green eyes that perfectly matched the silky sheath she wore. They were both elegant and sophisticated. "No one asked you to watch, Mother."

Oooh, Mother. Only rich people used that particular name and my insides started to sour.

"How could I not when my son is making such a display of himself?"

He snorted. "Newsflash, Mother, you are the only person who cares what these people think. I'll do what I want, with whom and when, got it?" The fire in his eyes and the tick in his jaw spoke to how agitated this encounter was making him.

"Preston, don't talk to me in such a tone." She put her hand to her chest, feigning shock even to the untrained eye.

"No, Mother, don't *you* talk to me that way. If you don't mind, we were having dinner." He back turned to me and grabbed my hand with a smile.

"Oh, please. I know you think this bartender is fun and worldly, but we both know she's all wrong for you."

His grip tightened around my fingers, and I kept silent. "Frankly, Mother, I don't think you know anything at all, especially when it comes to me."

"I know that Cynthia here would make you the perfect wife."

I froze, wondering for just a moment if I was some last hurrah fling before he married his perfect Stepford wife. But Preston scoffed and turned his gaze to the other woman, Cynthia. "That is never going to happen. Not ever."

"We'll see."

Preston smacked the tabletop with his fist, drawing stares that clearly made his mother even more uncomfortable. "Nothing you do will make me marry her, or any of the other brainless twits you send my way. The more you want it, the more I will resist out of pure fucking spite. Got it?"

She turned to me, eyes keen and cold as ice. "Sabrina Worthington, I'm sure you've heard of me."

"Not at all. Nina." I didn't bother offering my hand because it wasn't nice to meet her and I wasn't a liar.

"Well, Nina, I'm sure Preston seems like a good catch with his money and family connections."

Her words pulled a loud, unladylike laugh from me. "Money and family connections? Are you serious, lady? I'm with Preston for his body."

"Classy," she snorted in a way that said she thought it was anything but classy.

"About as classy as trying to force your son to marry someone because of her name and what her grandparents did."

"You don't want to tango with me, little girl. Trust me, you will lose."

I snorted. "Look lady, I don't even want to talk to you, but you interrupted a really hot kiss for this nonsense. And I don't know you, which means I trust you about as far as I can throw you." I sized her up. "Want to see how far that is?"

She gasped and stepped back, and I had to resist the urge to smile at how easy it was to frighten her. "Enjoy him," she sneered, "because this won't last long."

"Oh, I fully plan to enjoy him. Every inch of him, every day, and in as many positions as possible." I turned my heated gaze on Preston, who looked shocked and uncomfortable and a little turned on.

"You'll never fit in with his life. When Preston decides to stop playing around, he'll need a proper wife at his side."

"Mother, stop!" He stood up and got in his mother's face, which was totally fucking hot. "I love my job, and I won't change it for anything or anyone. When you understand that, we'll talk. Until then, have a good evening."

"But, Preston," she sputtered, clutching her invisible pearls and looking around at all the eyes on our little exchange.

"You started this, Mother. Now leave, or I will finish it."

She sniffed and turned, walking away with her head held high, ignoring the whispers and stares as she exited the restaurant. "Call me," the younger icy blond, Cynthia, said with a smile.

"Don't hold your breath," he snarled and took his seat. "Sorry about that."

"Don't be," I told him honestly. "We can't pick our parents, and as bad as she is, I've had foster mothers who make Sabrina look like June Cleaver."

Preston froze and stared at me, his look undecipherable. Then, he huffed out a laugh. "I don't know who to feel sorrier for."

"I have an easy fix for that. Instead of feeling sorry at all, we drink." I didn't give pity or accept it — pity helped no one. Drinking though, has healed plenty of wounded souls all over the world.

"Then we should do it right." Preston summoned our waitress to the table and in that moment, I caught a flash of the powerful man he could become. Might, in fact, become.

With the right woman at his side, just as his wicked bitch of a mother had said. I could see in him the man his mother wanted him to become, and suddenly, I felt like exactly what I feared I might be.

A girl completely and totally out of her comfort

zone, doing her damnedest to taint the golden boy. A girl hanging on to the right man for all the wrong reasons.

Preston was a great guy. He'd spent the night doing it best to make me feel comfortable when I clearly didn't belong. Would it always be that way, if by some stretch of the imagination we stayed together, with him working all the time to make me feel better?

It would get old soon, I knew, and what might have started out being cute and quirky would become annoying. Unbearable. He would resent me, and it would be impossible to live in a small town like Tulip any longer.

We toasted our sorry parental state with champagne and there, over the sound of bubbles, I heard it.

The other shoe, hitting the floor with a thud.

CHAPTER 20
PRESTON

"Hey Nina. I don't know why you're not answering my calls. Or my texts. But I'm starting to worry. Call me back."

It was a strange message to leave when we lived the kind of small town where it was near impossible to avoid anyone even when you wanted to, but somehow, Nina had managed to stay away from me for four days. Ever since our dinner had been interrupted beautifully by my mother.

I couldn't prove it, but I knew Mother's words had gotten to Nina and I knew I needed to see her in person so we could talk. With my shift over, I needed a nap, a meal, and a shower — not necessarily in that order — and then, I would go to Nina.

As urgently as I wanted to talk to her, sleep was a bigger priority after a couple of the longest days of my life. Several campfires and two different parties of lost hikers meant Nate and I had spent most of the past few days outdoors, on our feet. There were no casualties, though, which was a bonus — and not just because it would've added hours of paperwork to my shift.

I only had to work an extra hour to finish up the paperwork on all the rescues, which was, of course, always preferable to searching for bodies. Driving through town, I resisted the urge to stop for coffee, for breakfast at the diner, or at Nina's house. I was too tired to think straight. I needed to be at home. In my bed.

Of course, the phone chose that moment to ring. "Yeah?"

"You sound like a grumpy Gus."

"And you are too chipper for this early hour. What's up, Janey?" My foot hit the gas a little harder, hoping I could get home and honestly claim to be in bed before anyone asked anything of me.

"I need your help. Come to the park and use the Orley exit. Oh, and bring your uniform!"

"What—" I pulled the phone from my ear and stared at an image of Janey sticking her tongue out at last year's Fourth of July barbecue at Ry's place. She'd hung up on me. "Dammit, Janey!"

Calling her back only got me through to her

voicemail five separate times, and cursing my own bad luck wasn't helping. I didn't know if she was in trouble or someone else was, and that meant my shower and a few hours of shut-eye had to be pushed back a little longer.

Two miles before home sweet home, I swung a U-turn in the middle of the road and made my way to the park. The Orley entrance. Since I couldn't get ahold of Janey, I grabbed a first-aid kit and some climbing gear, hoping I wouldn't need even that much, and walked toward the park.

"Over here, Pres!"

I turned to see Janey and enough gear for ten photographers spread out between a crop of trees. "What the hell is going on, Janey?"

She frowned. "You look like crap."

"Yeah, well, I'm at the ass end of a three-day shift and I've been up for about forty-eight hours straight. I'd say it's a legitimate excuse." Instantly, her expression turned contrite.

"Why didn't you say anything? Oh, crap, you guys were out there with that group of lost hikers, weren't you?"

"Yeah. I didn't tell you because you didn't give me a chance, and I thought you were in trouble."

"Sorry. I figured it was best not to give you guys too much notice for the actual shoot. But now that you're here…" She let the words hang in the air and I stared at her with my arms crossed, waiting. "Ugh, don't give me that look, Preston, I saw you naked before you got hot."

My lips twitched but I was too tired to even grin. "Ditto, Janey." The shade of red coloring her face was enough to tease a laugh out of me, though.

"Have some java and stand here while I check the lighting."

I accepted the coffee, taking a few big gulps before I started to feel semi-human again. "What is all this?"

"This is how we make the light bounce where we want it to bounce." That was the only explanation she offered up, but it was more than enough at my current brain capacity. The only thing I could manage was turning here and there as Janey commanded from every spot imaginable.

"You're not taking pictures of my backside, Janey."

She snorted. "Of course not, unless you change your mind. But you won't be the only thing in the shot, in case you were wondering. It's called background."

"Smartass," I grumbled, which drew another laugh from her. With more than a moment to wander, my thoughts inevitably went to Nina and her recent strange behavior. No matter that she claimed everything was fine, that *she* was fine, I knew she wasn't.

"Yoo-hoo, Earth to Preston. What's going on with you today? And don't say you're tired, because I've seen you exhausted and this ain't it, my friend." Before I could catch even a hint of sympathy in her eyes, she ducked back behind the camera and continued to snap photos.

"Nothing is going on with me, other than doing favors for my friends."

"Yeah, right." She chuckled. "Look right at the lens," she commanded, then kept on snapping. "You talk while I shoot."

"You gonna take photos with me flapping my jaw?"

"Yep," she said quickly and took a few more shots. "It'll be easier out here with no one around to hear, plus, if you get emotional, there's no one around to see you cry."

"Except the number one blackmailer in Tulip?"

She shrugged, completely unapologetic. "Only when it's necessary."

Janey was true blue, only blackmailing you into something when it was something you should've said yes to without the coercion. So, I talked and told her all about the amazing dinner I'd had with Nina.

"Until Mother showed up with Cynthia St. James and got in her head. Who knows what it even was that got to her, you know?"

Janey nodded. "I can see how Sabrina might scare her off, she can be intimidating to those who don't know her. You just can't let her." She was down on the ground, snapping photos from half a dozen different angles. "She's not from around here, which means she doesn't know that Sabrina is more talk than substance. Talk. To. Her."

"I've been trying, but I've also been kind of busy saving people's lives, ya know?" More than a dozen calls and at least double that many text messages, and all I'd gotten in return were a few bland texts that said nothing at all about why she was pulling back.

"Try harder." The words were practically a growl, and it shocked the hell out of me. "Unless you really are just using her until you marry one of the socialites Sabrina picks out for you."

"That's not what I'm doing. I like Nina."

"Then try harder, Preston. She's not like the women who want you because of your name or your money, or the influence that comes with being a Worthington. A woman who likes you for you, with all that going on, is a keeper."

My lips curled at one particular memory. "She

told my mom and Cynthia she was with me for my body."

Janey snorted a laugh, as I knew she would. "I'll bet Sabrina loved that."

"I wouldn't be surprised if she tries to get her fired." Mother could be vindictive when she felt humiliated, and there was no doubt that's what Nina had done.

"I won't let that happen." Janey's godfather was the mayor — if anyone could pull rank over my mother, it was her.

But I wouldn't let it happen, either. It was past time Mother learned there were consequences to her meddling. "Thanks, Janey."

"None necessary. Nina stepped up and she's doing a damn good job, which means I can scoot out of town for the occasional gig without risking everything falling apart."

Nina was doing everything right to fit in to Tulip without changing the core of who she was. There was no way in hell I would let my own damn mother screw it up. "She'd be happy to hear that."

"No, she wouldn't," Janey said with a smirk. "She'd be happy to know it, but not to have someone actually voice it to her."

"That's true." For all her tough badassery, Nina

couldn't take a compliment to save her life. "I think I'll tell her anyway."

"Good. Now, do you think I can get you to lose the shirt for a few shots?" Her smile was hopeful, her eyes playful.

"Nope."

"Dammit. How about unbutton it and let it hang loosely, and I'll send one to Nina to seduce her?"

"Tempting, but no."

"Can't blame a girl for trying."

No, I couldn't. But it didn't stop me from wondering why the hell all the women in my life were so crazy.

CHAPTER 21
NINA

You're avoiding me.

That was the message Preston had sent me yesterday and, because I'm a coward, I avoided it.

Avoided looking at it a thousand times and avoided responding to it. Because, again, I'm a coward. I know I'm a coward and while I hate it, I also know I'm too much of a coward to do anything else.

In fact, I hate myself for being such a coward. For allowing a stuck-up bitch like Sabrina Worthington to get to me. Make no mistake, she was an expert manipulator, honing in on your weak spot in seconds and poking at it until you were ready to cry or risk prison to shut her up. But I had allowed her to get in my head, and that was on me.

Not Preston.

He didn't deserve the silent treatment, because he hadn't done a anything wrong. I had. And I owed him a pretty big apology.

The gods were on my side, as they say, since I'd been freed from the boot that morning and, before I'd left the hospital, I'd gotten Derek to agree to be one of the hometown heroes. One more and I'd have a hat trick for the day.

My next stop was the Black Thumb, where I was surprised to see Buddy and his big belly leaning against the bar. "You got time to lean, then you sure as hell got time to clean," I told him, mimicking his slow Texas drawl.

Buddy straightened immediately and scowled at me. "Very funny, little girl. You're looking better."

I smiled and kicked my leg up in the air. "Walking better, too. Know what that means?"

"You want back on the schedule?"

I nodded and leaned on the bar with a smile. "I do. Is that gonna be a problem?"

"Not for me, but you should know Sabrina Worthington showed her face in here and suggested I fire you."

That bitch. "You gonna?"

"Not a chance in hell. The minute she opened her mouth, she guaranteed I wouldn't ever fire you, girlie." He winked and pulled his famous clipboard from behind the bar. "Fill in the shifts you want and keep your mouth shut about it."

"Same to you, old man." I dropped a paper bag on the table, half clear with grease from the sandwich inside. "Stopped on my way back from the hospital in case I had to butter you up."

"To get your job back? Never. Just glad to have you back, I hate all these fancy damn drink orders."

I laughed and put an order in for me and Preston, too, hopefully. "Blue cheese and onion rings, and turkey bacon with sweet potato fries, please."

Buddy's gaze narrowed. "That's unexpected, but I'm happy for ya, Nina."

"Don't be, I already screwed it up. This is me trying to make it better, since we both have to live here." Though I was starting to understand the old western cliché, 'this town ain't big enough for the both of us.'

"I'm sure you'll figure it out, but do it on your own time. Can't stand the drama," he grumbled and walked away to place my order.

While I waited for the food, I sent a quick text to Preston asking him to stop by when his shift ended. I knew he would be tired, but I hoped dinner would be just the enticement he needed to hear me out.

"Here ya go." Buddy handed me a plastic bag with two paper boxes inside. "See you Friday."

"Can't wait! Thanks, Buddy."

Knowing Preston's mother had tried to get me fired pissed me off more, and reminded me of something I'd forgotten while I let her get the better of me. I hated rich bitches like Sabrina Worthington; she wasn't the first I'd had the displeasure of encountering and I doubted she would be the last.

Which only made the fact that I was in love with her son that much sweeter.

"You okay, girl?"

I blinked and turned stunned eyes on Buddy. "I'm fine, thanks. See you soon, Buddy."

That silent admission shocked the shit out of me. My legs could barely support the weight of my realization. I was in love with Preston.

Holy shit, I loved Preston!

And that made everything—the food, the impending apology, the hopeful reconciliation blended with the sad resignation of simply co-existing in the same small town—that much scarier. This wasn't just some fling that I could easily bounce back from. No, this was bigger. Deeper. More important.

I forced my feet to move back to my car and headed to my apartment, feeling happy and free to be able to take the steps without a limp. Without getting too tired, although wearing the boot that long had obliterated what little physical fitness I had left.

I pushed inside my apartment and took a quick shower, changing into jeans and a t-shirt for the conversation we needed to have. This wasn't about sex or seduction, this was about us. Me and Preston Worthington, a guy so far out of my league he thought he was the lucky one. But I knew the truth; I was the lucky one.

And I'd screwed it up.

So, I waited. And I waited. And waited. But when one hour, and then two and three passed, I gave up. He wasn't coming. I sulked.

I screamed.

I ate my food and then I scraped the blue cheese off his burger and ate it, too. Later, I finished off the onion rings.

When it became clear that he had no plans to respond or stop by, I locked the door, turned out the lights, and crawled in bed to do something I hadn't done since I'd lost Uncle Rudy.

I cried myself to sleep.

CHAPTER 22
PRESTON

"Who in the hell dives in without checking the depth first?" Nate shook off as much water as he could before stepping into the ATV we used to get to hard-to-reach locations tourists often got themselves stuck in, literally. "Idiots could have died."

I laughed and climbed behind the wheel. "They're lucky all they got was three sprained ankles and one broken one." The waterfall was beautiful, but it was called the Wishing Well Waterfall for a reason — the four-and-a-half-foot depth was ideal for making wishes, not diving into the icy water. "And I ruined my phone."

"Put it in rice. Fucking tourists," Nate grumbled.

It was a familiar song from those employed by

the Parks Service. Without tourists, we wouldn't have a job, but they sure made our jobs more difficult than they needed to be.

"At least they didn't spill any blood, or we'd be filling out forms all day instead of going home and gettin' some sleep."

"Can't argue with that." My bed was calling my name and I had just enough energy to make the drive home without crashing into anything or anyone.

But when I got there, there was an unwelcome visitor on my porch.

"What are you doing here, Cynthia?" Of all the unwelcome sights to face after a long shift when I was chilled to the bone, none was more unwelcome than Cynthia St. James.

Her lips spread into what I'm sure was meant to be a seductive smile, but her constant cosmetic work made it look more like a grimace as she stood with her tits thrust out, barely covered by her skimpy pink dress that showed off all the other physical enhancements she had made over the years, and a pair of shoes that made her legs look ten miles long. She probably came close to breaking her neck on her way to my door.

With her lips pouting in that way women thought was sexy, Cynthia slid her hands over her curves with a gleam in her eyes and flicked her blond hair behind her shoulders. "If you want to be chased, Preston, just say so. I'm happy to play the game, but this thing where you pretend to hate me is getting old."

How do you tell a girl that you weren't just pretending to hate her without sounding like a dick? "What gave you the idea I *wanted* to be chased?"

I was a man who preferred to do the chasing.

"Sabrina said you were a little reluctant to marry and that you might need convincing to settle down, but she assured me this marriage would happen, Preston." Her tone was crisp and clear, devoid of deception, and I sighed as some of my anger cooled.

It wasn't Cynthia's fault. My mother couldn't simply fathom a world where people didn't jump to do her bidding.

"Too bad you've been talking to someone without any decision-making authority on who I marry. Or don't marry." It would never be Cynthia, not if she was the last option in all of Tulip.

But Cynthia wasn't done yet. She notched her chin up into the sky and folded her arms over her chest. "And if she cuts you out of the will?" Her lips curled up again, this time in a cat-that-got-the-canary grin, like she'd trapped me.

Money was a surefire way to get the attention of

the idle rich. I didn't bother telling her that Mother had no control over my trust fund, it would only encourage her. "I earn a good living, Cynthia. Thanks for your concern."

"You can't possibly marry the bartender. Sabrina won't allow it. She'll disown you." She laughed like it was the funniest thought in the world, and that pissed me off. I hadn't been thinking about marriage to anyone. Not even Nina. But suddenly, it didn't seem so strange, so crazy, or so out of character.

Shit.

I laughed it off and pushed the key in the hole. "She did that when I chose my career path, which means I can and will marry whoever I please." I sighed as my eyelids slid closed. "I don't want to marry you, Cynthia, and there's nothing my mother can threaten or promise to change that. We're not right for each other, so please, move on to the next name on your list. Good luck."

Cynthia, ever the pragmatist, straightened her spine and nodded once. "Thank you for being honest with me. Good luck with the bartender."

I watched her leave, making sure her car was off my property before I locked myself inside the house and headed straight for a shower hot enough to singe my skin. The hot water on my sore, cold muscles felt amazing and, if not for the fact that I couldn't keep my eyes open, I might have stayed in there forever.

Dressed in nothing but a pair of boxers, I grabbed my phone and put it on the charger before I remembered it was completely waterlogged. Drying off the memory card as much as I could, I inserted it into the backup phone I kept because SAR crew were always on call; dead phones were no excuse.

After a few minutes, the phone lit up and began chirping and beeping, and I let out a sigh and a groan that was mostly relief.

I had missed a text from Nina. Asking me to stop by so we could talk. And it was sent almost twenty-four hours ago. "Shit!" She probably thought I'd stood her up, because that was exactly what I would've thought if our situations had been reversed. I wanted to talk to her, to explain everything.

But I knew I physically couldn't make the drive, so I sent her a message.

Tonight. Let's talk. About everything.

With the text sent, I fell backwards onto my bed and watched the ceiling fan spin in slow, lazy circles until my body grew heavy and sank into the mattress. I fell into a deep, dreamless sleep.

When I woke up ten hours later, there was just one thing, one person, one woman on my mind.

Nina.

CHAPTER 23
NINA

Today was a new day. I decided I would put Preston in the past where he belonged, right along with the rest of my baggage. I'd spent more time than I would ever admit to crying and feeling rejected. It wasn't the first time in my life I'd experienced that, but it had hit me just as hard.

I straightened the mess my place had become over the past few days. Schedules and binders sat on top of every flat surface, proving that I would be earning my second paycheck every bit as much as my first.

The calendar was the first big project and the biggest priority, but Tulip was a town that liked festivals, concerts, plays, and movies in the park.

Not to mention the town-wide block party in the middle of the summer.

That's where my attention would be from now on. Work. It gave me the means to take care of myself. Whatever the future held, I would be prepared.

For anything.

The phone rang and I groaned. Okay, so I was ready for *almost* anything. It was either Max or Preston and I was in no mood to talk to either, but this was the new and improved doesn't-get-ruffled-about-things-she-can't-control version of me, so I closed my eyes and tapped the screen blindly. "Yeah?"

"How did it go?"

Max.

My shoulders relaxed, proving I'd been more worried it might have been someone else.

"It didn't. He didn't respond and he didn't show." Each time I thought it or said it, the words hurt a little less.

"That son of a bitch," she growled. "What did he say when you confronted him?"

I squeezed my eyes shut tight, blocking out the embarrassment that washed over me. "I didn't and I'm not going to. Not showing up was as much an answer as him hearing me out and then telling me to go to hell."

"You don't mean that, Nina."

"I do. Look, Max, am I pissed about it? Yeah, but it was his choice and I'm going to respect it. No questions asked."

"You're a better woman than me."

I laughed at that. "I'm not, trust me. The difference is that I'm the one who screwed up. I should have kept it to sex only because that's what I'm good at, what I know. The mistake was thinking we could be more, and his silence was a big, beeping, red-flag reminder."

"That's crap and you know it." I could feel Max practically vibrating with indignation on my behalf and though I loved her for being so soundly on my side, it was completely unnecessary.

"You guys are good together, really good. He smiles more and he's more relaxed with you."

"That's the byproduct of regular sex, Maxine."

She barked out a laugh down the line. "Regular sex, what's that? It's been so long I think I'm like Barbie down there."

"That's a visual I didn't need," I joked, but I appreciated the effort since it took the focus off me. "I'm glad we're friends, Max."

"Me too," she sighed. "It was hard going for a

while, because you are one tough nut to crack, but I'm glad I kept at it. You're a good friend."

"I don't know about that, but I'm learning. And one of the things I've learned is that when you sound out of breath like that, you're busy in the kitchen. Need a guinea pig?"

She laughed. "Sure. We're having a tasting menu for dinner tonight."

"Oh, the exciting life you lead. I've never even had a tasting menu." It sounded expensive and likely far outside of my budget.

"Then you're in luck because tonight, we have a big spread. Come over around seven. I need to go; if I burn the caramel, you're cleaning the pot."

"Then go, woman, go!"

She laughed and ended the call.

I sucked in several deep breaths and touched the smile that still lingered on my face as I finally understood what Uncle Rudy meant when he talked about the healing power of friendships. I'd honestly always thought it was just a line for all the women who lined up to babysit on Friday nights, but as it turned out, he knew his stuff. Talking with Max didn't make the hurt go away, but it dulled the pain a little.

Baby steps.

Returning to the stacks on my coffee table, I focused on the calendars, adding everything that had already been confirmed. I made sure to include all the details, since I'd have to chase down the heroes for their photo shoots and promo for the calendar. It was nice to have something to focus on. Getting lost in work wasn't something I'd ever experienced, but there was a soothing quality about it that I enjoyed.

Until a knock sounded on the door.

I knew my luck had run out, and when I opened the door to find Preston scowling at me, I wasn't even surprised.

"I didn't get your message until this morning." The words rushed out of him like he'd been holding them in for too long.

I stared at him for a long, long time, just soaking in his masculine beauty. Preston was a good man and, someday soon, he would marry a woman that wouldn't make his life miserable. That woman wouldn't be me. Still, it was nice to look at him for a while. "Okay."

"Can I come in?" He looked so earnest with his hands shoved in his jean pockets, showing off strong biceps and delicious triceps.

How could I say no? "Sure." It would be easier if I just listened to whatever it was he felt he had to say, and then we could get on with the ignoring each other portion of our lives.

Preston stepped inside, just past me, and I caught a whiff of him, a fresh shower scent and that undeniable aroma that was all Preston. My gaze ate up his long muscular legs as he moved around my space, taking in the binders spread out over the sofa and coffee table. "My phone is waterlogged, and..." he began absently and walked into the kitchen. I followed him.

"That's okay, Preston. You don't need to explain."

"The hell I don't." His expression was dark and cold. Angry. "I wasn't blowing you off. I wouldn't." I believed him. It wasn't in Preston to be mean. If it was, he'd have told his bitch of a mom to go to hell ages ago.

"I know." I sighed and took a step back before he had the chance to reach out and touch me. "At least, I think I do."

"Then what's with the distance?" His smile was predatory but, thankfully, he stayed on his side of the room.

"There's no distance. This is just a conversation, remember?"

His lips spread into a grin and he raised his hands. "What did you want to talk about?"

"Nothing, I changed my mind. But since you're here, we can—"

"Bullshit."

His words were like a slap in the face. "Excuse me?"

"You heard me." One foot moved forward, but Preston didn't advance. "Bullshit. You wanted to talk about something. Over dinner."

"That was yesterday. I've changed my mind." It was mostly true, so I didn't know why I had to fight the urge to fidget so hard.

It was a useless effort. Preston saw it and pounced. Arms crossed, he was wearing his most smug smile. "What was for dinner?"

"Nothing special, just takeout."

"From where, Nina?"

Why did I have to go and fall in love with the most stubborn man on the planet?

"What difference does it make?" I asked. "The food is long gone, and so is my desire to have that conversation with you."

Yesterday, I'd been feeling brave and bold and ready to take on the world, but one little setback and I was crying like a teenage girl. That was all the proof I needed that this relationship stuff wasn't for me.

"It matters to me. What did you order from Buddy for dinner?"

I shouldn't have even been surprised. "Burgers."

His shoulders relaxed and his smile brightened enough to illuminate my whole apartment. "Blue cheese for me?"

"Maybe, I don't remember."

"And onion rings." This time it wasn't a question, just a statement to accompany his big, all-knowing grin.

"Okay, so what? You want to rub in the fact that I clearly read things wrong between us? Go right ahead, Preston. It's my fault for thinking you were better than that."

Why I felt so itchy, so uncomfortable with this assessing gaze on me, I couldn't say. But the fact that I lashed out, completely unreasonably, spoke volumes.

"That's not what I'm doing, and you know it." Though his smile had disappeared, the self-satisfied gleam in his blue eyes remained.

"Then what *are* you doing?"

When his big body began to move this time, it was with purpose. Serious intent. Preston's steps were slow and deliberate as they approached me, stopping only when barely a breath stood between us. "I'm trying to get the truth out of you, because you are confusing the hell out of me."

Join the club, buddy. "What difference does the truth make, Preston, when we're all wrong for each other?"

"I disagree," he stated as his hands firmly gripped my arms.

"No, you don't. You're a nice guy and you think saying so makes you a bad guy. You can't argue with facts."

"Whose facts? Yours?" He barked out a laugh that was somewhere between bitter and amused. "Or my mother's?"

"Just plain facts, Preston." I sucked in a deep breath and let it out slowly, begging with my eyes for him to understand. "What happens when you get tired or too old to work your physically taxing blue-collar job, and you want to go back to your one percent upbringing? Tell me exactly where a high school graduate who tends bar fits into that life?"

His expression transformed from serious to amused in a flash, and just as quickly, I felt my hackles rise. Then, a laugh escaped. I struggled to get out of his hold, but his grip was tight. Strong.

"Nina, you nut, I'm already rich. Half of my trust fund released when I turned twenty-five and the other half comes when I turn thirty or get married, whichever comes first."

What?

"What, no other ridiculous reasons to lob my way?"

Oh, he was so smug, I didn't know whether to smack him or kiss him.

"It's not ridiculous." It wasn't. These were perfectly reasonable concerns that any woman would have. "I'm being cautious."

"Scared. My big, bad, tough girl is a coward." His smile turned affectionate as he sifted his fingers through my hair. "Who'd have thought?"

"Of course, I'm a coward, I've never been in love before!" The instant the words were out, my heart stopped and my eyes darted wide open. Just like my mouth. "I, uh..."

"Didn't mean to say that," he finished for me. "I know you didn't mean to say it, but did you mean it? Do you love me, Nina?"

Yes. Hell yes, I did. "Doesn't matter. We're not right for each other."

His smile stretched from ear to ear. "You do." Big hands cupped my face and I watched, fascinated, as he leaned in and pressed his lips to mine in a soft, gentle kiss. I sank into him; my body refused to listen to my brain where this man was concerned.

Things were just getting good when he pulled back. "We *are* right for each other."

"Why do you say that?"

"Because I love you. And as hard as you're working to find a reason that we won't work, I'll work ten times as hard to prove to you that we do work. We will."

"You can't know that," I insisted, heart racing even more as this dream edged closer to being a reality.

"Do you love me, Nina."

"Yes. I am in love with you. Happy?"

His blue gaze sparkled with contagious joy. "Hell yeah, I'm happy. Thrilled, actually. You?" His eyes stared right into me, penetrating my soul. I felt him deep inside me.

I grinned. "Terrified as hell, but yeah, happy. I think."

It felt a lot like happiness, but I'd only had fleeting contact with the emotion so I couldn't say for sure.

"I'm happy. I love you."

Saying those words was scary as hell, but the look on his face was a moment I knew I'd never forget.

"I'm happy to hear you say that."

Then his mouth was on mine, a little rougher

this time. Hungrier and so intense it stole my breath. His hands were everywhere, spearing through my hair and squeezing my ass. Pulling me close, where he was long and hard against my belly.

"So glad," he growled against my mouth, making me laugh.

"Me too," I admitted. "But are you sure? This is going to piss off your mother. Big time."

I shuddered to think of all the ways she would come up with to terrorize me and try to run me out of town, like in those spaghetti westerns Uncle Rudy had loved so much.

"She'll get over it," he said, then smacked a kiss on one side of my jaw and then the other. "Or she won't. She can't affect our happiness if we don't let her, Nina."

"It's just that easy, huh, Worthington?"

"If we want it to be, damn straight it is."

He flashed that boyish smile and kissed me again.

"I don't care about any of that, Nina. I care about you. I love you and I want you. Me and you, together — how does that sound?"

"Sounds pretty good to me."

I was still scared as hell, but the idea of loving Preston freely, of accepting his love and letting myself be happy, was as appealing as it was terrifying.

"Great. And when you're ready, we'll discuss moving in. And marriage."

I let out a squeak of surprise, but before I could tell him he was moving a little fast and getting ahead of himself, his mouth crashed down on mine in a kiss that was as effective as a bomb at getting my attention and holding it.

All I could focus on was Preston — his hands, his mouth, his hard body pressed into mine.

"I'd love to wait, but I can't," he panted as he picked me up and lay me across the kitchen table, where he proceeded to kiss my body until I shook with need.

And then, much, much later, Preston made slow, sweet love to me.

It was the start of what I hoped would be a pretty great love story.

EPILOGUE

Preston

"Is all this really necessary?"

How in the hell did I let Janey and Nina talk me into making a bigger fool of myself, again? Standing in front of the fountain in my SAR uniform with my arms crossed made me feel like a wannabe super hero. Or Captain Morgan. It was a toss-up, at the moment.

Janey sighed and rolled her eyes before she disappeared behind the camera again, snapping photos like I hadn't said a word. "Yes, Preston, it really is necessary."

"You look sexy as hell, babe!" Nina stood about eight feet behind all the camera and lights, smiling bright and doing her best—and her job—to make me feel like a sex symbol instead of an idiot.

"Yeah, thanks." I gave her a wink and she blew me a kiss, making me happier than a man should be that she'd hurt herself that day in the park.

"Yeah, babe, you look sexy as hell," Ry called out from right beside her. "For an old man."

"Why are you even here?"

Ry bust out a laugh, not even reacting when Nina smacked him in the gut. "I'm here for moral support."

I didn't buy that for a minute, but Janey snapped her fingers to get my attention before I could say a word. "What is this for, exactly?"

"Nina, can you talk him into taking off his shirt for a few shots?"

Janey was relentless. I felt bad for all the other so-called hometown heroes who still had to do all this.

"Yeah, Nina, come talk me into it."

She smiled at the challenge in my tone and came forward with a smile. Over the past month, since we'd cleared the air and made the decision to move forward together, Nina had been a wonder. A delight. She was more open with her affections, especially in public, and she was more confident in our love.

"Do you want me to talk you into it," she whispered, nibbling my earlobe.

"I want you to try," I told her with a groan when her tongue slipped into my ear, forcing my eyes closed so I was completely at her mercy.

"You do?" she asked, moaning as she pressed her curves up against me, letting one hand roam under the heavy-duty SAR work shirt.

"I'd love to see a photo of you all sweaty, with your muscles peeking out of this green shirt. Seeing all the women drool over you and knowing you're mine," she whispered. "All mine."

"Yeah?" I liked where this was going, and I didn't give a damn that we might have an audience.

"Uh-huh. Then I'd stare and imagine all the dirty things I'd like to do to you, and the things I'm dying to have you do to me."

Every word, every syllable was accompanied by the stroke of her hands, the flick of her tongue, and the fan of her breath. "Maybe I'd even eavesdrop to see what kinky things the single women of Tulip come up with and I'll do that to you, too."

"All right, fine. Ten shots and that's it." My voice was rough, like I'd swallowed a bag of rocks and washed it down with whiskey.

"Thanks," she whispered with a quiet laugh as she stepped back. "I love you, Preston."

"Love you right back."

She let out the same tiny gasp she always did, as if she just couldn't believe that I loved her too. It was total bullshit, but it had a way of making me feel ten feet tall — and it made me want to show her in every way possible just how worthy she was. Hell, the truth was, I didn't deserve her.

"Good to know." She stepped back and winked. "He said okay, Janey."

"I said ten shots," I clarified with a low, dark growl.

"Make it twenty," Ry called out, mouth split into a grin that was far too amused.

"Twenty what?" asked a tiny voice that belonged to a little boy with curly blond hair.

Ry froze and looked down at the boy next to him, who gazed up at Ry with a wide, chocolate smile. "Twenty photos. Big, manly photos."

"I do twenty, too!" He jumped up and down, nearly falling over in his excitement before Ry saved him from a face full of cement.

"Whoa, there, champ. Slow down." The kid hung onto Ry, smiling at him in amazement like he was a real-life superhero. "What's a little guy like you wandering around out here all alone?"

"He's not alone." The voice belonged to Penny Ford, a Tulip transplant who'd taken on the job of assistant to the mayor almost a year ago. I didn't know much about her, and as far as I knew, no one did.

"Penny," Ry said, his voice reflecting the recognition written all over his face. "This little wanderer is yours?"

"He is," she said simply, one brow arched in a challenge.

There was an entire universe of tension and unspoken emotions between them, and I grinned.

"What's going on there?" Nina leaned in and whispered as she tucked a hand into my back pocket.

"I think I've just identified Ry's mystery crush."

And now I understood his hesitation. Penny was a few years older than Ry and she seemed to be a serious woman, a sharp contrast to his easygoing nature.

"Ry, aren't you gonna introduce us to your friend?"

It probably made me a jerk to give him a hard time when he was so clearly transfixed by this woman with her all-black outfit, and tight bun pulling all of her hair backwards, but that's what friends are for.

He glared at me, and I decided not to comment on the hint of pink coloring his cheeks.

"Guys, this is Penny, she's Mayor Ashford's assistant."

I was immediately forgotten as Nina and Janey made a beeline for Penny, giving me plenty of time to corner Ry and find out more.

"So, this is the woman keeping you from dating. Interesting."

"I date," he insisted, but without any of his normal fire.

"You're a terrible liar, and I hear that's a great quality in a boyfriend."

"What's a date?" the little boy asked, popping his head up just late enough for us both to realize he wasn't sleeping.

"When you make time to hang out with people you like," I told him easily. "What's your name, kid?"

"I'm Mikey and I'm five." He held up a hand with five wiggling fingers and a broad smile.

"I'm Preston, and this is Ry." He put his little hand in mine and gave it a solid shake for a five-year-old. "Nice to meet ya, kid."

"Mice to meetcha, too!"

If there was an award for adorable, this kid's misspoken words and boyish excitement would win hands down.

"Did you know about this?"

Ry shook his head, still looking a little shell-shocked. "Nope, but I'm more worried that I'm not worried about it."

That would worry me, too, but I kept my mouth shut. "If you need any help, you know how to find me."

"If you and Nina ever come up for air."

"We will. Soon."

"Trouble in paradise?"

I shook my head. "Just the opposite. As we speak, all of her things are being moved to my place."

We'd talked about moving in together a couple of times, but her lease was up tomorrow and she'd only keep procrastinating if I let her.

"That sounds like a fight you don't want to have, my friend."

Mikey squirmed out of Ry's grasp and Ry let him down gently, not taking his eyes off the little boy.

"The argument will be short-lived, but the making up won't be. Play your cards right and you'll know exactly what I mean."

He snorted and shook his head. "First, I've got to show her I'm more than just some immature kid with a crush."

"If anyone can do it, Ry, it's you."

"Yeah, thanks for the confidence, but I'm almost

at my limit of rejections." Still, his eyes never strayed far from Penny.

I smiled. Watching this drama unfold might make this hometown heroes calendar nonsense worth it.

The End.

PREVIEW: MIDLIFE FAKE OUT

She was the one with the bottomless brown eyes that always seemed to be on the verge of tears that never fell.

Those eyes had called upon all of my protective instincts.

But that had been too much responsibility for a high school boy.

I hadn't wanted or needed that kind of responsibility.

So I'd rebelled against those instincts, and did the opposite of protecting her.

I bullied her.

PROLOGUE

Derek – 2 Months Ago

A buzzing sound started to my left, and I flipped over to get the hell away from it. I didn't know what time it was, but the fact that I was still sleeping after the most epic awards show after-party meant it was too damn early for phone calls. But the buzzing didn't stop, and worst of all, there was a cold spot on my bed where a really hot model should have been. My eyes snapped open and I pushed off the bed, scanning the room for any trace of Sasha, or Satya, or something equally as trendy.

"Hello?"

Silence met me as the phone continued to ring. The bedroom floor no longer held a pair of tiny panties. Sheer tiny panties, if I recalled correctly, and I usually did recall, because I wasn't the kind of guy to forget what type of lingerie I tore off with my teeth. Names and jobs? Sure. To call? Almost certainly. But never lingerie. Ever.

I hurried out of the bedroom and down the hall where my black slacks sprawled across the top three steps. I distinctly remembered a long green dress with sparkles on it being somewhere near the bottom of the staircase, but now it was gone too. So were the sky high heels that capped off the longest set of legs I had ever seen. I went left at the bottom of the staircase, and the coffee table still held a half-empty bottle of champagne, two glasses beside it, one stained with a red lipstick imprint. My jacket was on the back of the sofa, along with the bowtie I'd left to hang around my bare chest, because that's what people expected of Derek Gregory, the heartbreaker of The Gregory Brothers trio. Ryan was the moody and sensitive songwriter, and Roman, as the youngest, was the goofball bad boy. We all had our roles, and I'd played mine perfectly for decades now.

I retraced my steps towards the kitchen, which was of course empty, because everyone knew models didn't eat. But there was a note. I smiled and strolled over to the counter.

"Thanks for a good time, Derek. You more than lived up to the hype. *Xoxo – Sascha.*"

I smiled even wider because she was a perfect woman. Looking for a good time with no strings and no expectations, and gone before the awkward morning after, where I would have to explain that I wasn't looking for anything serious, while a woman stared at me with tears swimming in her eyes.

"So did you Sascha, so did you."

In the big empty Nashville mansion, the only sound was my stupid phone still buzzing upstairs on my nightstand.

I took the stairs two at a time, wondering if Ryan or Roman had found themselves in the wrong type of trouble, which rarely happened, but rarely wasn't never. I quickened my steps at the thought that it could be something wrong with our father, GG, or worse, our sister Lacey, who recently decided to become an investigative journalist covering stories in chaotic regions of the world.

"Yeah, what is it?"

A familiar sigh sounded down the line, and I pinched the bridge of my nose a moment before my agent, Brody's angry voice sounded. "So you haven't been abducted by aliens or models, and you're not lying dead on the side of the road," he grumbled. "I guess I should thank the lord for tiny favors. Very tiny."

I rolled my eyes because I knew that tone. "What

did I do now?" Usually I managed to balance the line between lovable bad boy and asshole perfectly, but sometimes I stepped over that line. Sometimes I jumped over it by a mile. "Well?"

"You mean other than offending our core audience with some attempt at comedy that just came off as sexism and misogyny? Is that not enough for you, Derek?"

"You're going to have to give me more details, because all I did last night was accept a few awards, dance all night, and made Sascha moan my name until the wee hours of the morning. So tell me Brody, how have I offended our beloved fans?"

"Stop me when this starts to sound familiar yeah? *She needs to be barefoot and pregnant soon, so you can get her back in the kitchen where she belongs.*"

I froze at those very familiar words. "Yeah they're familiar. I sent that exact text to my new brother-in-law. Yesterday. Was my phone hacked? Don't worry I don't keep nudes on there," I assured him with a laugh.

"Derek," he roared over the phone. "You idiot, you beautiful, talented fucking idiot. You didn't send that to your brother in law, you sent it out to your ten million followers."

"Ten? Try twenty-three million, not that I've been counting." I tried to be active on social media, to keep the fans engaged with photos of me and my brothers, me just living my life.

"Even worse. You did hear the words I just read back do you, didn't you? Barefoot and pregnant? In the kitchen where she belongs? To our mostly female fanbase!"

"Brody it's not that big of a deal. I'll explain that it was a private message and a joke. I'll even do a video with my sister to show them." This will blow over in a day or two, it always did.

"No you won't. I don't want you to do a goddamn thing Derek, except what I tell you to do. What I need for you to do is go away. Just for a little while. Lay low and go on a social media hiatus until I tell you otherwise."

"What? You've got to be kidding me, Brody. It was just a joke!"

"It was the wrong type of joke at the wrong time, and it offended *everyone*! Go back to that Podunk town you're from and keep a low profile, Derek. Can you do that? For the sake of your career, and if not yours, then your brothers."

"Shit, you're serious."

"Yeah Derek, I'm serious. This whole situation is serious, and I need you to take it seriously."

I worked too hard on my career to lose it now over some silly joke. "I'm listening. Go home and stay away from the spotlight." My shoulders fell in disappointment. "Anything else?"

"No," he sighed in relief. "I need to get with the public relations team and figure out how in the hell to fix this mess. Don't do anything until you hear from me. Got it?"

"Got it."

There must have been something in my tone, because when Brody spoke next, his tone had softened. "This isn't the end of the world Derek, but it will take some finesse to handle it. Just sit tight, and for once in your life, do as you're told. Tell me you can do that."

"I can do that Brody. My career means everything to me, you know that."

"I do, but I also know you're a stubborn asshole when you want to be."

"I'll close up the house now and head to Carson Creek today," I told him, completely defeated.

"Good. And stay away from all press and social media for the next few days, will you?"

I nodded even though he couldn't see me and dropped down onto my bed. Either that or my legs gave out as the gravity of the situation settled on my shoulders.

"Yeah, okay. Sure." I ended the call and sat on my bed for what felt like forever, contemplating how in the hell I'd ended up here after such a spectacular night.

We'd won three awards last night for our last album, including Song of the Year, and today here I was.

Exiled.

CHAPTER 1
BELLA

Early mornings were my favorite time of day, always had been. The world was quiet and peaceful as the earth tilted to meet the sun's golden rays, and only a few brave souls were awake to see the first beauty of the day. It was, and had always been a private time, a time for me to gather my thoughts and prepare for the day ahead.

Now that I was officially a farmer—again—of my own free will this time, early mornings and to do lists were a necessity. For now I was a one woman operation with the help of a barely teenage boy, who was now, technically, my son.

It hurt to think about Nicola's premature death. She was my best friend, my sister in all but the biological sense, and now she was gone thanks to that unforgiving bitch known as cancer. Her death had left me and her son Everest alone in the world, forced to cope without her sunny disposition and ability to see the positive in any situation. Now it was just us, two cynics who still hadn't found a way to do more than exist without her.

That's what Carson Creek was for. It was meant to be a change, a reset for both of us, but more of a homecoming for me. I grew up here in this town and on this farm. I tilled and watered the land, fed the animals, plucked the crops and sold them all over the state. I loved farm life, it was in my blood, and I'd always dreamed of taking over the place once Ma and Pa retired. Then high school started, and the bullying, the name calling, the stares and the pointing. What fifteen year old girl didn't want to wear makeup and look pretty for hormonal teenage boys, right? Even worse than my distinct lack of desire to impress said boys, my sister would argue that I went out of my way to make sure they weren't interested, but the truth was you could only wash your hands so many times to get the dirt from under your nails. Too many hours in the barn, and not even two showers could completely shake the smell of hay. And what was so wrong with the scent of hay anyway? Without it we wouldn't have food and nourishment, but that only made me more of an outcast.

So instead of sticking around and taking over York Farm, I hightailed it out of this town as fast as I could and claimed the college scholarship that waited for me in Texas, where I'd met my best friend, Nicola.

And now she's gone.

My phone beeped and the screen lit up to remind me that quiet time was over. "Ev, breakfast is ready!" I called upstairs to the sleeping teenager, because I'd learn one month into our first nine months together that yelling was more effective than a gentle shake to wake him from his slumber. The boy slept like the dead, a skill I envied each and every day. I waited and stared at the ceiling until movement stirred above me, before I finished my coffee.

Ten minutes later Everest made his appearance. At just thirteen, he was already the same height as me. But he was at that stage where his limbs were the size of a grown man's, but he was still very much a boy, with long gangly limbs, thick shaggy black hair that looked like it hadn't seen a comb in six months, and skin as smooth and as clear as a baby's. His mother's gray eyes stared back at me, and I couldn't help but smile at the heartbreaker in training.

"You're staring again, Aunt Bella."

"Yeah, I know, and I'm not sorry at all. I was just thinking that one day soon you're going to be such a handsome stinker." He already had the makings of it, and when his growth spurt hit and his baby fat melted away, young adult women of the world would lose their minds.

Everest smirked back at me, a blush stained his cheeks. "Yeah? What am I *now*, chopped liver?"

"Nah, I wouldn't say that. Right now you're a cute stinker, emphasis on stinker. Hungry?"

"Always," he laughed and grabbed the coffee pot.

"Still too young for this," I reminded him.

Everest shrugged and poked his head into the fridge where he emerged with a bottle of orange juice. "Better?"

"Water would be better, but that is acceptable."

"Water isn't going to give me the energy I need for a long day working the fields." It was a good attempt at a guilt trip, but it wasn't good enough.

I laughed and put one hand on my hip. "Working the fields? Hardly, more like feeding some animals and cleaning some stalls, which shouldn't take more than a few hours. When you're done you can go into town and see about making some friends." We'd been in Carson Creek for a few months now, and he'd barely left the farm or made an effort to mingle with the other teens in the area.

His shoulders stiffened at my words. "I don't need to make any friends, Aunt Bella. I'm fine here on the farm. I like it here."

I nodded, because I understood the urge to hide in the face of grief. "This is your home, Ev. You will always belong here, and that won't change if you go out and make a few friends. Have a little fun."

"Not yet, Aunt B. Okay?"

I nodded. "Okay, not yet then. But soon. You don't want to start school as the new kid."

"Fall is months away. I'll be fine."

"Okay fine. If you'd rather spend time with your super cool aunt, instead of swimming with girls at the lake or sneaking beers at the movie theater, who am I to argue?" I laughed when he rolled his eyes, enjoying this time together, because I knew that one day soon, he would wake up and view me as the enemy.

"You know if this whole farming thing doesn't work out you might have a second career as a standup comic."

"Har-har. Thanks for the vote of confidence, kiddo." I pressed a kiss to his cheek and ruffled his hair before I grabbed my phone and headed towards the back door. "I'll be fixing the fence on the south end for most of the morning, and I have my phone. Take yours with you, just in case." I called instructions over my shoulder for what felt like the hundredth time, and then I was gone, out in the already warm and sunny day.

I smiled as I hopped in my shiny blue pickup truck and headed to the fence that probably hadn't been fixed since the last York left the farm about ten years ago. It was good to be back on the farm, this time around I was older, and supposedly wiser. I didn't need to make friends or connections for my social development, I'd given up on love well before the ink dried on my second divorce, which meant I only had to do two things in this world, raise Everest into a good man, and make this farm a success again.

Both jobs were daunting, and I wasn't even sure I had it in me to do either one of them well, but those were the only things I wanted to do, which meant failure was not an option.

I had a plan. For York Farm and for Everest.

The farm was the easier task to tackle, so I focused on that while I grabbed pliers and twisted the wire around the wood posts, replacing as necessary. The land was big by family farm standards, but there was enough room to grow squash, soybeans and tomatoes on the main plots. Eggs from the chickens would sell well, because they always did, and if the trees on the west end of the property were still good, maybe apples and cider in the fall. The vertical farming buildings were already producing, so the farm could start making a profit sooner rather than later, which would help replenish the money I'd spent to fix this place up and make it livable for me and Everest.

I had a stack of parenting books in my nightstand drawer. Admittedly, that wasn't the most exciting thing to have in that particular drawer, but the books were a greater necessity than battery operated lovers. I now realized that audio books might have been better, since most of my time was spent outdoors, and that way I could multi-task, learn the best ways to parent a child who'd lost his mother, while catching up on my never-ending to-do list.

Mending the farm fence was a hell of a lot easier than the other fence I would have to mend someday. I wasn't much of a fence-mender in the real world, more of a fence burner. Hell, even that wasn't accurate. The truth was that I was more of a barn burner, I didn't just burn the bridge, I blew up the entire structure. It was my modus operandi because life was easier to deal with that way. Scorched earth meant there was nothing to return to, or attempt to fix later.

"What a joke," I muttered as I examined my handiwork. The fence looked good, but it was the only fence likely to actually get mended. At some point in the future, before I die, I would have to reach out to my four siblings, Abel, Amara, Andora and Alex, and do something or say something. Maybe an apology or something, I didn't have a clue what would do the trick, which meant it wasn't important enough to make it onto my to-do list.

Yet.

Everest likely needed more family than just me, and I had family members in abundance. Maybe the York family could be for him what they had never been for me. Or maybe I just hadn't given them a chance.

I guess my family would go on the list sooner rather than later.

Some days being the adult, the logical and reasonable one, really sucked.

CHAPTER 2
DEREK

It hadn't taken long for boredom to set in once I got back to Carson's Creek. I lasted one week staying with Ryan and Pippa. They were disgustingly in love and I was happy for them, but I didn't need to see my brother and sister-in-law making out while trying to enjoy my morning coffee. And my niece Ryanna was as cute as they came, but she was curious as hell, and when she couldn't explore she proved to have Gregory lungs.

Roman's place was empty, so I stayed there for a few nights since I'd sold my house in Carson Creek last year. That was a good decision at the time, since I didn't spend much time in my hometown, and when I did, I had three siblings and an ornery father to stay with. But my current stay in Carson's Creek wasn't quite working out as I had hoped. After one too many eager groupies showed up at my baby brother's door, I knew my social media restriction wouldn't last long.

So I did what any reasonably wealthy and completely exiled rock star would do.

I bought a farm. Or was it a ranch? It was a giant plot of land with several smaller buildings on it that I hadn't bothered to look into as carefully as my business manager would have liked. It was out on the outskirts of town, which made it perfect in terms of privacy, and there was enough room that I could probably turn one of the buildings into a studio. This exile might be the perfect time to start building my credentials as a producer, at least that's what I told myself, but seven weeks in, and I hadn't even called a contractor. Or hired anyone to tend to the overgrowth which was out of this world.

I thought about asking my neighbors next door, since the rumor in town was that someone had actually purchased or rented the York Farm, but I hadn't seen any evidence of their existence beyond a shiny truck and crops growing day by day. *Great, they were actual farmers,* which probably meant early to bed and early to rise.

The neighborly thing, the southern thing to do, would be to go over there and introduce myself.

Maybe offer some muscle once in a while and hope they would do the same for me.

Another time, maybe. I needed, no, I wanted to get the studio built as soon as possible. It would give me something to do, and it would keep me out of trouble until Brody reached out to say I could make trouble again, and do it publicly. I got up and dumped my lukewarm coffee down the sink, I then went about my daily ritual of discreetly checking the internet to see if the women of the world still hated me, and—yep—they did. Instead of stewing over it and cursing the world for my bad luck, I headed outside, determined to scope out the perfect studio space.

The building closest to the main house would be ideal for convenience, but I could put in a small unpaved path if one of the other buildings proved better suited. It was so quiet that I could hear mosquitoes whizzing by my ears, birds chirping in the distance, even the crunch of overgrown foliage under my boots.

It was too quiet.

But I heard a vehicle in the distance, close enough that it was either a visitor for me, or someone at the York Farm was out and about.

My phone beeped with a message from Roman. *"Where the hell are you?"*

"I'm at home. Grounded."

That's exactly what it felt like. I was back to being fourteen and forced to sit in my room and do nothing, not one damn thing, because I'd gotten caught doing something stupid. *Some things don't change*, I thought and smiled to myself.

"We're here," was the next message that came through.

I made my way back to the front of the main house, an act that took even longer than walking the property of my Nashville mansion. Both of my brothers stood on the front porch looking around at the property, probably wondering what in the hell I was thinking.

"Hey, what are you guys doing here?" Not that I wasn't happy to see them, but I hadn't had any visitors in weeks. "Didn't even know you were in town," I told Roman.

Ryan shrugged and ran a hand through his long blond hair with a sheepish smile. "Pippa thought you might be going nuts out here by yourself and made me come."

"Gee, thanks man." I snorted and punched his shoulder.

"I would've come out if you had asked, but you're not exactly the begging type." He wasn't wrong. I didn't need a group to amuse myself, at least that's what I told myself, but I had been going a little stir-crazy out here on my own.

Roman shrugged and clapped me on the back with a playful smile as he gestured to the land before us. "I just wanted to lay eyes on the old hovel, see what kind of dumbass trouble you got yourself into now."

"It's hardly a hovel," I told him and shoved my elbow into his side. "The place just needs some tender loving care, which I plan to give it. With the help of a landscaper and a contractor." Even as I said the words, a vision of what the place would look like came to me.

"A contractor?" Ryan's arched brows nearly disappeared into his hairline. "For what exactly?"

I nodded for them to follow me around to the back of the house. "Afraid I'm going to open up a place to rival Dark Horse?"

"Hell no," he growled. "Nina is happy where she is, so anyone you could get would be a poor imitation."

I rolled my eyes. Nina was a damn fine chef and woman, but I had no desire to run a restaurant. "I'm going to turn one of the buildings into a studio, produce more tracks, maybe some albums for other artists. What do you think?" My brothers and I were close, very close, but we weren't the touchy feely sort to talk about our feelings until our voices went hoarse.

Ryan grinned. "Yeah? That's a good idea. Plus, the main house is big enough if you want to put the artists up yourself."

I hadn't thought about that, but it wasn't a bad idea. "Like those old artist communes back in the day," I mused, suddenly liking the idea more and more.

Roman snorted. "Of course you would decide to do this after my first album is done and on the shelves. But it's a good idea, a good way to keep busy until your current shit storm blows over."

"Don't remind me," I grunted. "One little mistake and I'm being tarred and feathered." I still couldn't believe it, and I was pissed off. But I promised Brody I would be smart and that I would listen. "Anyway..." I said in search of a change of topic and coming up empty.

"Meet the new neighbors yet?" Ryan asked with a smirk.

"Nope. I guess they're real farmers or something." I did think it was strange that I hadn't even caught a glimpse of them yet. "Or vampires, possibly ghosts."

Ryan rolled his eyes. "Pippa was right, you are going crazy."

"Maybe the ghost farmers are just good at hiding from the misogynistic rock star," Roman mused and pointed to a figure off in the distance.

I followed the direction of his finger and let out a small gasp, because it was an actual person. "Unbelievable." I guess I had started to believe the place might be empty. Carson Creek specialized in gossip, but they didn't always get it right.

"Let's go introduce ourselves," Roman said and started towards the fence before anyone else had agreed. Typical youngest kid, always did whatever the hell he wanted.

"I guess we're going to meet the neighbors," Ryan said with a knowing smile that normally would have set me on edge, but nothing in my life was normal right now and it was all because of social media.

No, it was my fault. Plain and simple.

By the time we got to the fence Roman had already introduced himself, though it probably wasn't necessary because the kid already knew him.

"Oh wow. I love The Gregory Brothers, but your new album is incredible. Been listening to it on a loop since it came out," the teenager with black floppy hair had an awestruck grin.

Roman stood a little taller at the compliment. "I would offer a signed CD, but I wouldn't even know where in the hell, um heck, to get a CD anymore. But I'll definitely get something to you."

The kid laughed and shrugged. "You don't have to do that."

"You kidding? Without fans I wouldn't be shit, I mean hell," he sighed and scrubbed a hand over his face. "You know what I mean right kid?"

"Yeah," he nodded. "I do. The name is Everest, by the way." He finally noticed me and then Ryan with wide gray eyes. "Holy shit, do you guys live next door?"

"I do," I told him and stepped forward with a handshake. "I'm Derek, and I just bought the place. Haven't seen anyone next door at all."

Everest nodded and glanced at the property with a critical eye. "What are you planning to do with the land?"

"My first plan is to get the land cleaned up so I can see what my options are, but I'm going to turn one of the buildings into a recording studio."

"Cool," he nodded and looked around. "I can help clear the land if you want."

"Yeah?" I didn't know, given the current state of things, if that was such a good idea. "Why?"

He shrugged. "My aunt keeps talking about going into town and making friends. If I have something else to do, especially a job, she might lay off awhile longer."

I frowned. "You don't want to make friends?" What kind of teenager didn't want friends, especially a good looking kid like him that could easily be very popular?

"I just got here, and things have been rough. My mom passed away, and I'm just taking it easy for a while." He scanned the grounds once again and turned to me with those gray eyes that looked as if they'd seen too much. "I spotted some peach trees on the south end of your property, if you're interested in tending them, they look to be bearing fruit." The way the kid breezed over the dead mom information called to me, I'd done the same when we lost our mother.

I smiled at his mature way of speaking. "You grew up on a farm?"

"Nah, but my aunt did, and she knows all kinds of stuff."

"So why aren't you helping her?" Roman shoved his hands in his pockets and leveled Everest with a look.

"She only lets me feed the animals and clean their living areas because she wants to make sure she can handle the workload when I become the most popular kid in town." He snorted his opinion at that aspiration. "Anyway, you know where I'll be if you decide you want some help. It's a big job."

We all smirked at how easy the kid was with us. "Everest, why did you guys choose Carson Creek?" There were bigger towns and bigger farms throughout the state.

He shrugged at first, and then lifted his eyes to the blue sky and blinding sun. "She grew up here. Said she didn't much like it here back then, but that it was a great place for us both to start over, so here we are. Oh and this is her family's farm."

No. it couldn't be. The universe couldn't be so cruel to me, not now when I was exiled to my hometown. The universe would not trap me beside my biggest regret, would it?

There were five York kids, and three of them were girls. It could just as easily be Andora or Amara, but my gut knew that it wasn't. It was the svelte York sister, the one with the bottomless brown eyes that always seemed to be on the verge of tears that never fell. Those eyes had called upon all of my protective instincts. But that had been too much responsibility for a high school boy. I hadn't wanted or needed that kind of responsibility. So I'd rebelled against those instincts, and did the opposite of protecting her.

I had bullied her. Badly.

"One of the York girls," Ryan mused. "Which one?"

"Bella York," a rich feminine voice answered as she came to a stop beside Everest. She was as beautiful as ever. Gorgeous with her long limbs, strong and lean. Her white tank top showed off her shoulders and toned arms, a pink bra peeked from behind one of the straps. But her legs were the real superstars, encased in denim that looked damn near painted on. A floppy hat sat on top of her thick brown hair that hung halfway down her back, or would have if the wind hadn't picked it up and swirled it around her body. She put a hand on Everest's shoulder and smiled. "The Gregory Brothers. Hey Ryan. Roman." She didn't say my name or even look in my direction, and I wasn't at all surprised.

"Bella York," Roman purred and leaned in with an appreciative smile. "You always were a pretty thing, but holy hell woman. I'm of legal age now," he reminded her and wiggled his eyebrows.

Bella laughed, and the sound was thick and rich. "Thanks Roman. And congratulations on your solo and group success. You guys are all over the place."

"We took a risk, and it paid off." Ryan shrugged like it was no big deal. "What are you planning to grow?"

"Quite a bit actually. Soybeans will be our

biggest crop, there will also be squash and tomatoes, and hopefully some apples from the orchard. I also have a vertical farm with plenty of herbs and leafy greens. A lot of stuff," she said with an embarrassed laugh. "Sorry."

"Don't be," Ryan assured her. "I own Dark Horse, it's a high end restaurant in town, and my chef Nina loves to come out and pick fresh food. She would love this."

I watched as she chatted easily with my brothers, and wondered to myself how it was possible that she had gotten even prettier over the years. She was still willowy with this innately delicate look about her, but now there was also a strength about her, inside and out. "It was great to see you guys, a real blast from the past. But I need to get back to it," she said and thumbed in the direction over her shoulder. "Tell your chef to come by anytime to check the place out. I'm happy to show her around." She took a few steps back, brown eyes smiling wide at my brothers before she turned to Everest with an affectionate smile.

"What about me?" I shouldn't have said anything. I should have just left it well enough alone. She didn't like me, probably hated me, and she had good reason to ignore me completely. But that just wasn't my style.

Annabella York froze and turned slowly to level me with an icy glare. "What about you?"

I took a step forward and licked my lips. "Am I welcome anytime?"

She flashed a sexy smile, and I swore my knees gave out a little. She was hot as hell fully clothed, and I couldn't help but imagine what she would look like in nothing at all.

"You, Derek Gregory are welcome, never. Not ever, even if there's an end of the world disaster. Unless of course you have a fondness for the taste and feel of shotgun slugs."

"Ouch," Roman groaned and then laughed.

With a pointed look at me to make sure I got the hint, she turned and walked away, long legs eating up the space quickly.

My brothers roared with laughter at her insult, looking at me with questions in their eyes that I refused to answer. "I can't wait to hear that story," Ryan said around a loud guffaw.

Even Everest laughed. "Wow. I'm pretty sure Aunt Bella hates you, and she likes everyone. *Everyone*," he emphasized. "Sorry," he added with a shrug. "It was nice to meet you guys. All of you." He waved and walked off, shaking his head with an amused smile.

As soon as Everest was out of earshot, Roman

laughed even more loudly. "What the hell was that about man?"

"Ancient history," I growled and walked away from the fence, putting as much distance between me and Bella York as possible. With her so close, her hatred so palpable, it didn't feel all that ancient. It just felt like another thing that I would have to apologize for.

Eventually.

Some day.

Later.

Bella & Derek's story continues in Midlife Fake Out.

ALSO BY PIPER SULLIVAN

Midlife Fake Out: Bella & Derek

Midlife Love Story: Carlotta & Chase

Midlife Love Affair: Lacy & Levi

Midlife Valentine: Valona & Trey

Midlife Do Over: Pippa & Ryan

Healing Love

Dueling Drs, Book 6: Zola & Drew

Rockstar Baby Daddy, Book 5: Susie & Gavin

Unfriending the Dr, Book 4: Persy & Ryan

Kissing the Dr, Book 3: Megan & Casey

Loving the Nurse, Book 2: Gus & Antonio

Falling for the Dr, Book 1: Teddy & Cal

Curvy Girl Dating Agency

Forever Curves, Book 8: Brenna & Grant

Small Town Curves, Book 7: Shannon & Miles

Curvy Valentine Match, Book 6: Mara & Xander

Misbehaving Curves, Book 5: Joss & Ben

Curves for the Single Dad, Book 4: Tara & Chris

His Curvy Best Friend, Book 3: Sophie & Stone

Curvy Girl's Secret, Book 2: Olive & Liam

His Curvy Enemy, Book 1: Eva & Oliver

Small Town Protectors (Tulip Series)

That Hot Night, Book 12: Janey & Rafe

To Catch A Player, Book 11: Reece & Jackson

Cold Hearted Love, Book 10: Ginger & Tyson

Hero Boss, Book 9: Stevie & Scott

Dr's Orders, Book 8: Maxine & Derek

Mastering Her Curves, Book 7: Mikki & Nate

Kissing My Best Friend, Book 6: Bo & Jase

Undesired, Book 5: Hope & Will

Wanting Ms Wrong, Book 4: Audrey & Walker

Loving My Enemy, Book 3: Elka & Antonio

Bad Boy Benefits, Book 2: Penny & Ry

Hero In My Bed, Book 1: Nina & Preston

Accidental Hookups

Accidentally Hitched, Book 1: Viviana & Nash

Accidentally Wed, Book 2: Maddie & Zeke

Accidentally Bound, Book 3: Trish & Mason

Accidentally Wifed, Book 4: Magenta & Davis

Boardroom Games

His Takeover: An Enemies to Lovers Romance (Boardroom Games Book 1)

Sinful Takeover: An Enemies to Lovers Romance (Boardroom Games Book 2)

Naughty Takeover: An Enemies to Lovers Romance (Boardroom Games 3)

Boxsets & Collections

Small Town Misters: A Small Town Protectors Boxset

Misters of Pleasure: A Small Town Protectors Boxset

Misters of Love: A Small Town Romance Boxset

Misters of Passion: A Small Town Romance Boxset

Kiss Me, Love Me: An Alpha Male Romance Boxset

Accidentally On Purpose: A Marriage Mistake Boxset

Daddies & Nannies: A Contemporary Romance Boxset

Cowboys & Bosses: A Contemporary Romance Boxset

About the Author

Piper Sullivan is an old school romantic who enjoys reading romantic stories as much as she enjoys writing them.

She spends her time day-dreaming of dashing heroes and the feisty women they love.

Visit Piper's website www.pipersullivan.com

Join Piper's Newsletter for quirky commentary, new romance releases, freebies and contests.

Check her out on BookBub

Stalk her on Facebook

Printed in Great Britain
by Amazon